About the author

After a career as a creative thinker in technology and business consulting, especially in Japan, the USA and the UK, I retired to the New Forest to enjoy life, leisure and the opportunity to spend time indulging my interests in all sorts of new and challenging activities. I have a lovely wife to whom I have been married for over fifty years and three sons whom I encouraged to go out and experience the world, with the result that none of them now live in England!

ZENDUST

DEREK NEWTON

ZENDUST

Vanguard Press

A CIP catalogue record for this title is
available from the British Library.

ISBN 978 1 80016 381 2

*Vanguard Press is an imprint of
Pegasus Elliot MacKenzie Publishers Ltd.*
www.pegasuspublishers.com

First Published in 2023

**Vanguard Press
Sheraton House Castle Park
Cambridge England**

Printed & Bound in Great Britain

Dedication

This book is dedicated to all the sad addicts, their families and the millions of people worldwide who are helping addicts and their families to a better life in the hope that, one day, ZENDUST will become a reality.

Chapter 1
A Star is Born: John Douglas and ZENDUST!

The phone was ringing, interrupting his dream. "Good morning, Dr Douglas, this is make-up, will you be ready in thirty minutes?"
What a crazy idea... make-up... I must be dreaming. He rolled over and back into sleep mode...

The phone was ringing again. He was still more asleep than awake after the flight from London. He was forty-two years old and for the first time in his life he had thoroughly enjoyed the luxury of first-class, especially the champagne,and the fact that the cabin staff kept referring to him by name and asking if he had everything he desired. *Almost,* he had thought at the time as the attractive flight attendants fussed around him. Much better looking, he thought, than the ones he was used to seeing at the back of the plane in economy class, where they were little more than waitresses.

It rang again and again. The girl from make-up sounded ever more insistent. Coming to his senses, he wondered again whether it was real, was he really there or was it all a dream? He, Dr John Douglas, Drug

Control Research Professor, waiting for TV make-up, of all things!! And in the best hotel in New York, where the world's press was assembling downstairs to hear what he had to say… this was going to be his day, he could feel it in his bones. He was exhilarated already!

He roused himself and went through to the shower, a marble-faced luxury spa-bath with TV, fragrances, soaps, gels of every possible kind, towels as thick as volumes and a view across to the UN Building and the river beyond.

I could easily get used to this kind of lifestyle, he thought to himself, *a bit different to home, and better!* The view of the UN building glistening in the morning sunshine was no coincidence, he knew. Countries in the Orient and South America who cultivated the deadly flowers were sending their delegations to the morning's press conference, as were countless countries throughout the world whose people were afflicted by the curse of deadly drug addiction, with all its consequences of wasted lives, the national and futile expense of trying to control the flow into their borders, and the treatment centres that were a desperate attempt to save their countrymen, for whom there really was little chance of regaining their lives.

'ZENDUST', Douglas' new treatment, was the key to removing the pernicious, all-consuming and irresistible need for the next fix for addicts. It promised a release from the slow, inevitable, awful death sentence of drug addiction and a return to a new and normal life for millions. He had his successful case studies, his trial results, his proofs… Today was the day he was going to tell the world.

The phone rang again. *God, this is bloody annoying,* he thought and snatched it to his ear.

"Room service, sir, would you care to order some breakfast?"

"No," he retorted and slammed the phone down. He had enough butterflies in his stomach already at the thought of the day to come, without stuffing himself with one of those enormous hotel breakfasts of doughnuts, bagels, jam, bacon, eggs and God alone knew what else.

"I never could believe they could eat that much at breakfast," he said to himself.

Choosing the most expensive-looking sachet of moisturising body shampoo, he immersed himself in the spa, luxuriating in the warmth penetrating his whole body from the foamy water, and contemplating with enormous pleasure the internal warmth he felt when he thought about what he had to say to the world this morning.

Soaking in luxury, with the jets on full blast, he thought again of home, picked up the phone next to the bath, dialled and waited for Val to answer, back in their small semi-detached house not far from the university in Birmingham. No one picked up the call and he remembered it would be about two in the afternoon and Val would be at the boutique she ran with a friend or at the drop-in addiction clinic at which she volunteered when the boutique business was slow. She knew a little of his work and she only visited the addicts as a means of being able to talk to him in the evenings about something that would interest him.

It's a real pity she didn't come with me, thought John as the answerphone clicked in: 'John and Val, leave a message!" He had always thought the answerphone reply was a bit abrupt and unfriendly but Val had said anyone from whom they really wanted to hear would know the message and ignore the rather peremptory answerphone response. Like many others before him, he imagined, he put the phone down without responding to the machine's abrupt note and without leaving any message. He was busy anyway. *Sod it, it will be make-up time soon,* he thought.

Fifteen floors below on the executive floor, two others were waking. They were only sixteen years old and could look ahead now to a life free from addiction. The needle scars on their wrists were fading. It was Douglas who had given them back their lives. It really was a kind of resurrection for these two who, a few weeks earlier, had been on the sad and lonely pathway to death by drugs, without a hope of turning back. Today they would tell their stories too.

Make-up rang again.

"I'm on my way," he said as brightly as he could, remembering the champagne. Sixty minutes later he was there spruced up, made-up, psyched up, and primed by the chairman of his company to ensure he maximised the impact of today's presentation, hence raising the company's share price and attracting new investors. Douglas had been instructed in no uncertain terms to make sure he mentioned how much the company had invested in the research to date, how there was an urgent need to ensure that the results were brought forward without delay, how much that might cost, and what profits might be forthcoming.

"Oh, and by the way," the chairman had said, "don't forget to mention how many crackheads there are out there who will be our customers."

Douglas was waiting for the signal to take the podium and glanced through the side curtain.

The ex-crack cocaine contingent was there, the black kid from the Bronx who had been his first success, the mother who had left her family, the kids who had sold the deadly little packets from the backstreets of downtown to the leafy suburbs of upstanding communities, the deadbeats and no-hopers of society. They now sat neatly in the front row of the Hyatt Gold room awaiting their deliverer. This motley crew owed him their health and sanity. They were his case studies.

The room was packed with the world's media: TV cameras by the dozen, operators adjusting their lights and cameras, satellites live with red lights winking, presenters preening in readiness, directors scanning the monitor banksand worrying. It was essential that every moment should be captured.

He was news with a capital N.

Government representatives sat comfortably with their coffee, waiting and watching with a mixture of expectation overlaid with disbelief and a desire to be reassured that this curse on society was to be lifted. Douglas held the prospect of lifting from their shoulders a problem that had blighted their finances, police forces and prisons for years.

Pharmaceutical corporate executives fingered their expensive watches. Time was money to them, but today's event might be worth billions of dollars, so they waited and fretted and murmured to their colleagues and secretaries on their cell phones. He was mega-bucks if the truth about him was real.

They were all gathered now.

DARC and Douglas himself had been pestered for information ever since the news of a solution to the drug-addiction problem had filtered out, but they had agreed to maintain an embargo until today, the launch press conference. This had built up expectation and maximised the impact, exactly as Kent and Solomons planned.

Douglas and the other execs from DARC, Solomons and George Kent, had met several times to plan the launch. Everything had to be perfect on the day; there would be no second chances. George Kent was the chairman of DARC, the Drug Addiction Research Charity Inc and seventy-five per cent owner.

DARC's attention to data security had been so tight that they had booked a whole floor in the hotel for their exclusive use and had it swept for bugs. No one was going to get a jump on, or any exclusive information, before DARC said so.

Dead on ten a.m., George Kent, Dan Solomons and John Douglas walked onto the raised platform of the Hyatt Conference Suite. The room was packed and expectant, an electric atmosphere, just as Kent and Solomons had planned.

Taking the centre chair, George Kent sat for a moment, looked around, recognised several faces and friends, noted that there seemed to be someone from every race, colour, and country, and then stood to begin proceedings.

The TV lights were intense and the news director gave him the signal that the networks were live.

"Good morning, ladies and gentleman," he said, "welcome to this press conference on behalf of the Drug Addiction Research Charity Incorporated.

"I would like to introduce Dr John Douglas, Lead Scientist on this Programme, to my left and on my right is Mr Dan Solomons, Chief Executive Officer of DARC.

"Thank you all for coming. We have, as I think you have all guessed, some amazing news for you. Today's news will touch vast numbers of families, communities, and, most importantly, individuals throughout the world. We are pleased to see so many nations represented here today. Our news today will be welcomed by everyone in every nation across the globe. What we have to tell you today will create major business opportunities for companies able to work with us on commercialisation. Governments, too, stand to make major savings on healthcare programmes."

Kent paused for a few moments and took a drink of water from the glass in front of him, deliberately raising the tension of expectancy from his audience, then continued:

"And, what is this momentous news? It is that DARC and our lead scientist, Dr John Douglas, have developed a cure for drug addiction. We have named our innovation 'ZENDUST'.

Why ZENDUST? Because the karma and the feeling of peaceful tranquillity that comes from the ancient practice of Zen is exactly what we can give to the millions of addicts out there in every city of the world. They are truly the walking dead, with zero life expectancy. They need a release and a rebirth to normality. They will need ZENDUST... "Or, as we say in DARC, 'It is ZENDUST or zero life'."

Kent paused to let the drama of this announcement have its impact on the minds of all those listening in the Hyatt Conference Suite and of all those tuned in to the live telecast in countries far and wide.

He knew that those six words would be the catalyst for headlines in the newspapers and media. It might even become the soundbite of the century...

There was dead silence in the room and, he was pretty sure, in the rooms of countless viewers to CNN and their TV network partners. He had grabbed the attention of the entire watching world.

"ZENDUST has been developed under DARC's Speculative Research Programme and we would like to thank our many sponsors and investors for the confidence they have had in our strategic research efforts. Naturally, the formulations are the subject of patent applications right now and are secret and we will not discuss confidential technical details today.

"I would now like to introduce our lead scientist, Dr John Douglas, who will present our case studies and demonstrate our success. Dr Douglas will focus his presentation on the trials and results we have achieved to date. We are sure these trials will give you all here today, and all those watching and listening, the most exciting evidence that you could possibly have imagined about how ZENDUST will change the world of illegal drugs. "This is, without doubt, a great day for mankind. With that in your mind, I would like to hand over to Dr Douglas. His presentation will confirm everything I have said about the opportunity ZENDUST provides to resurrect the lives of drug addicts worldwide."

John stood and moved over to the microphone in front of the TV cameras, as he had been directed. This was it.

He had called home the previous night to give Val the news about the timing of his presentation so that back home in England, they could share his big moment. Val had the TV going as she prepared the evening meal for herself and Annie.

"Quick, Annie, Dad's on the phone," she called. Annie was up in her room, preparing, Val thought, for her final college entrance exams.

"I'm busy right now," Annie called down, "I'll catch it all later on the video. Anyhow, if it's all that stuff about his work at DARC then I've heard about it endlessly from Dad."

With that, Annie shut the door and got back to her latest examination of herself in front of the bedroom mirror. *Looks pretty good to me*, she thought, and then propped her study book on the bed in front of her. She was actually feeling pretty good about the forthcoming exams; the motivation to get away from home and live life to the full was a powerful incentive. Val was busy too, she had had a good day at the boutique, been late back from the supermarket and there was a load to put away. "I'll catch John's TV talk on the video too," she thought, turned off the TV and opened the freezer door.

In New York, John took a drink of water, cleared his throat, calmed his nerves for a moment, and began the most important few minutes of his life. He had practised his presentation numerous times, in front of Kent and Solomons, and in front of a mirror by himself. At last, it was the real thing. His moment!

"Good morning, ladies and gentlemen and thank you, Mr Kent.

"I agree that this is truly a wonderful day for the world and I would like to give you a brief history on how we come to be here today with ZENDUST. "Some months ago, DARC agreed to sponsor my research on a novel approach to the drug addiction problem and I would like to record my thanks to George Kent and Dan Solomons for their support.

"As you have heard, our objective was to make ex-addicts out of addicts. My approach was directed at finding what caused the incredible urge that addictive drugs generate in users. It is this urge for the next fix, not the immediate effect of the drug, which causes the addiction. You may have thought that the need for the next fix was because the effect of the drug was so good, and I thought that too until I began to break down the biochemical actions of the various highly addictive drug categories.

"In the course of this comparative assessment, I was able to identify certain common constituents of highly addictive drugs, which were quite different in the effects they had on the user. In other words, I was able to see commonality in some of the biochemicals present in the hard addictive drugs which are the cause of so much misery worldwide.

"I focused on the hard-drugs sector, such as crack cocaine and heroin, as these present the most severe addictive problems. As a result of the study, I was able to determine that the need for the next fix was not entirely a function of the pleasurable effect of the individual drug. There was some common element that stimulated a need for the next fix.

"My next step was to isolate this element that I have called 'the next fix need component'. If that could be isolated, an inverse action chemical might be possible, and 'next fix need' would become a thing of the past. In other words, we would overcome addiction.

"There would be no devastating and uncontrollable urge for the next fix. This results in a freedom from the urge, the need and the addiction. This desperate urge disappears. This is the key to ZENDUST. Freedom from addiction. It is not appropriate here today to go into the details of the biochemistry involved. Rather, I would like to demonstrate that we have succeeded in our efforts by showing you some before-and-after video clips of our trial group.

"Can we run the video now please?"

With that, Douglas sat down to a silence of rapturous and focused attention such as he had never experienced in all the lectures and presentations he had made over the years. The room lights dimmed and the video clips flickered and began. The audience were treated to a series of clips showing the trial group of absolute no-hoper serial addicts, hooked on a variety of drugs, being transformed over a period of several weeks into a group of normal human beings, free of the addictive madness which had dominated their lives for so long. The happiness on the faces of his trial group shone brighter and brighter through the video clips as the addictive urge waned, and remembrance of a life without addiction returned.

Joey Jones, the heroin mainliner, was shown being picked up off the streets of London, filthy, unconscious, a mangy dog his only company, needles strewn around. Now he was shown with his arm around his sister, clean, smiling, happy, renewed.

Cathy was picked up from a line of worn-out prostitutes, looking only for the next quickie to pay for the next fix. Now she was reunited with her child, a bonny boy, obviously delighted to see his mum again, especially as she now loved and wanted him after months of blank indifference to anyone or anything except her addiction.

As he watched these stories and thought about all the others he had seen as he had been working on ZENDUST, Douglas thought of his daughter Anne back home and thanked God she wasn't into hard drugs.

Next was a young kid from America Douglas had picked up in a casualty ward where he lay under resuscitation, his arms peppered with jabs. He had the biggest and brightest smile now that you could imagine. He radiated happiness. The other examples were just as gripping. The TV images were compelling.

For his trial group, it was a kind of resurrection to life from a living death. The happiness on the faces of their friends and families must have been similar, or so

Douglas had often thought, to the way the disciples must have felt when they saw Jesus Christ risen from the dead, on Easter Day. His addicts had all been effectively dead and now were returned to life. Real-life resurrections. Douglas had been their personal saviour.

The clips faded, and John Douglas stood again at the rostrum.

"Ladies and gentlemen, I think you must agree with me that faces tell stories, and those faces you have just seen tell us that we have successfully achieved our objective. We have indeed made ex-addicts out of addicts. ZENDUST truly restores life to those with no life because of their addiction to hard drugs.

"The problems of addiction are worldwide and critical for addicts, families, friends, and governments. You here today, and all those watching, will understand that it is vital that we now have to move forward as quickly as possible to major trials, government safety regulation authorisation, and commercialisation. Not for our sakes, but for that of all those gripped by addiction, possibly dying at this moment, and for all their friends and families caught up in the terrible tragedies that follow.

"For example, I would like to introduce to you all today just one of our case clients. Joey, will you step forward?"

The skinny kid stepped out into the limelight, full of nerves, but aware of what a change in life he had attained.

"My name is Joey Jones. I'm just a poor kid from a poor family, no education, lots of problems in school. My friends were the local gang, and we looked for respect but no one had any for us. Drugs were easy to get; we could make big money. Easy. But the fixes had to get better and stronger. Next thing, it was a life of burglaries, muggings, anything to get the money what we needed every day to get a good fix. It was a treadmill to death..." He paused for a moment, as he had been told in the practice session; this was drama of the most human and awful kind and the media were transfixed.

He carried on after a moment. "But I was one of the lucky ones. Now, I am off that treadmill to death. The most wonderful day of my life occurred during the ZENDUST trial and it was the day I woke up without the devastating and uncontrollable urge for my next fix. I was free of the urge, completely free of the need for the next fix. I had been liberated from addiction. The desperate urge had gone, I was free, for the first time since I could remember, I could start to live again. This is the key to ZENDUST, it truly means liberation from addiction..." Again, he paused, letting the words sink in.

The whole auditorium was hanging on every word which came from this kid who, like millions of others around the whole world, should be dead.

"This man," he said, pointing to John Douglas, "is my deliverer. I would indeed be dead by now if not for him. He gave me a new chance of life. ZENDUST has been my salvation."

He sat down.

Douglas only added "Thank you Joey and thank you all for your attention," and he sat down to a stunned silence. The video clips and Joe's testimony had been the most dramatic demonstration of ZENDUST.

Applause spread throughout the audience. These were hard-headed folk not easily drawn to spontaneous appreciation of another person's efforts. This was different, everyone recognised that Dr John Douglas had delivered everything that he had promised in the pre-conference briefings. They stood, applauded, shouted and cheered. CNN were delighted, this was real-time news to attract the world's audiences, just as they had hoped.

In the few brief minutes of his presentation, Douglas had propelled himself from obscurity to international renown. He had achieved greatness.

My God, he thought to himself, *I can't quite believe I have really done it this time. It's absolutely fantastic. Hope Val and Annie are watching.* Kent and Solomons mentally counted the millions of dollars that would flow in to DARC.

"What a bit of luck, I never thought Douglas had it in him" said Solomons.

"Neither did I," breathed Kent.

DARC shares would skyrocket. Kent and Solomons calculated the value of their stock options, and both achieved a warm inner satisfaction that was better than either of them ever got from sex. They had both tried enough varieties of that to know.

In Medellín, Colombia, Juan Carioli, patriarch of the family's cocaine business, sat in his home, looked past the TV tuned to CNN, and contemplated long and deeply on what he had just seen. For sure, he was not about to let some crackpot scientist ruin the trade. He called his son Carlo in Miami; he would know what to do about this.

Carioli and his family had grown incredibly wealthy by satisfying the cravings of addicts. They were one of the five families that controlled the growing, harvesting and processing of cocaine in Colombia.

He had started small time in Miami, driving fast boats loaded with cocaine from his farm in Colombia into deserted beaches all over Florida. The family now employed others to do the risky work while they enjoyed a life of luxury in Medellín. Juan Carioli was now getting on in years and enjoying the easy life he had secured on the backs of the addicts who needed a daily fix of what his business readily supplied. At a good price, of course!

John Douglas would not be allowed to upset the Carioli family lifestyle. Juan Carioli was a survivor; others who had stood in his way now lay dead, buried and quickly forgotten. *This Douglas may well have to end up the same way*, was his uppermost thought as he looked back on the CNN newscast. He could rely on his son, Carlo, in these sorts of situations. Carlo had ensured the elimination of many a do-gooder who had been inconvenient for the family's business. He was the enforcer. And very efficient.

The phone rang loudly, interrupting his train of thought on what might become of Douglas.

"Hello Father," said Carlo. "I had to call you; I knew you would have seen the news about this ZENDUST stuff. This is a matter that might seriously threaten the business for our family." Carlo Carioli was sitting in his office in downtown Mami, looking every inch the Harvard-educated business executive, in his dark-blue trousers and gleaming white button-down collared short-sleeved shirt.

Juan Carioli reacted as he always had done to problems like this, "Do we know anything about this guy Douglas? Has he a wife? Or children? We need to get something over this guy and this ZENDUST crap," he spat. "'ZENDUST gives new life', what crap! Douglas will be lucky if he has any life when we... Maybe we should just kill him and be done with ZENDUST; what do you think, Carlo?"

"Just give me time to think on it. This is big news. We need to talk. We need to see what the other big families think of this. Will you speak to Gomez and the others?"

"When shall we meet?"

Chapter 2
Annie's liberation

Annie got out of bed. Looking briefly at the inert body still lying on the bed, she shook her head. She gathered her senses, wondered who he was, and came slowly back to reality.

What the hell was that stuff? she thought, as she rubbed the sore patch on her arm where the needle had gone in. She went out to the toilet, feeling sick, but nothing would come. Sitting there for a few minutes, she looked at the mirror and saw herself looking back, black-haired, green-eyed… a little pale, a bit unkempt, but still pretty cool she thought.

She was now a college student; she was free and liberating herself from of all her past inhibitions as fast as she could. She knew all her best friends would have skipped the morning lecture on *Philosophy and the 20th Century*. To Annie, it really was the most tedious subject you could ever imagine and she couldn't believe that she had really opted for Philosophy and English when she had qualified for college three months ago. John and Val had been very proud of their daughter Annie when they had dropped her off at the college. This would be the making of her, they had thought happily, a college degree, a good job in the future, nice boyfriends and girlfriends. Away from all those bad influences at home: kids with nothing to do; rich parents who never had time for their kids; the local drug problem on the streets.

They had driven down to the college together with all Annie's stuff packed in boxes, bags and whatever came to hand. John and Val had kept on at her to get packed up but as usual, things were left to the last minute. Annie was really only interested in packing up her hi-fi, the mobile phone and her outrageous collection of coloured mascara, lipsticks and hair dyes. She specialised in dark reds and blacks and deep blues.

Val had said before many times, "These don't suit you, Annie," but Annie was always one to go her own way and do her own thing.

As they said their goodbyes at her new room at the college, Val had said discreetly, "Be careful with all those young lads, Annie, you know what I mean. Dad and I want to be grandparents one day but not just yet!"

John was equally discreet. "Annie, you know about the work I do with drug addicts, and all the terrible things that can happen. Please take care and don't take any pills or anything worse. Have a few drinks and leave it at that. If others want to get stoned then let them. They will regret it, believe me, I know. Look after yourself."

Annie smiled her usual smile when her parents talked to her like that, said, "Of course," kissed them both, waved them away, went into her new room, on her own, and shouted, "Hooray, freedom at last!"

Life as a nice quiet daughter at home, the apple of her parents' eyes, was over.

I can do what I like, when I like and with whom I like and as often as I want to, she thought deliciously. Annie was indeed about to change in the most dramatic way, but not as John and Val would like.

To Annie, her academic subject was quite irrelevant to her lifestyle ambitions. She had only chosen it because almost no one else had applied and hence she could gain a place quite easily at the college in London. The choice had certainly worked out fine for her. It was a boring subject, but college life was great.

The three months had passed so quickly since she sat her exams, passed, and, to her great joy, got the place at college that enabled her to achieve her objective—an independent life without Dad, and particularly Mum, forever bickering and criticising her friends, dress, habits, late nights and just about everything she really enjoyed. She had taken to college life with uninhibited enthusiasm. Aiming to take part in everything, do loads of different things she had never had a chance to do at home, make new friends, experience new sensations, enjoy her freedom. Anything she *could* do she was definitely going to try.

It was fantastic for Annie to meet so many new friends, especially those who had already lived a much more liberated life than she had managed at home. She was dying to try all the experiences that her new friends knew so much about already. Little did she realise that dying for these new experiences was to draw her into nearly dying *from* these experiences. No such thoughts would, however, impact on her mind in these first few months of liberation, as she set about living life to the maximum she could possibly achieve. Free and casual sex was one of Annie's first priorities for new experiences.

Tonight, she chose her loose sweater and jeans, and no bra letting her full breasts hang loose, exactly what she wanted to attract some good-looking guy. Her mother would have been shocked, she knew, but she wasn't there and Annie could do exactly as she wanted. Putting on plenty of her blue eye shadow, off she went to the Fresher's Party ready to get laid without delay. Of course, it was easy. She had a few beers and got tipsy, kissed the guy she had only just met, let him fondle her breasts for a bit, and then said, "Shall we go back to my place?"

He couldn't believe his luck and he followed her back to her room where she promptly stripped naked, pulled down his trousers and lay on the bed ready. It only lasted a few moments; she was so disappointed. She lay there naked for a while, on top of the bedclothes and completely exposed, relishing the freedom to do what she wanted and behave outrageously if she wished. The guy was asleep, and spotty on his back and down his bum as she looked at him. Really, a bit of a chinless wonder.

Ugh, thought Annie. She got dressed and went out.

Her first few partners had all come, literally, in moments or so it seemed to Annie, and gone without much in the way of pleasure for her. Sex hadn't been as good as she had hoped and orgasms just never came. Not surprising really, she analysed afterwards, as her student partners were pretty inexperienced as well. Surely, she thought, there had to be more to be gained from her new freedom than she was getting from all this frivolous febrile fucking. She had even stopped showing off her figure so much by changing the clothes she now wore. She was sick of being targeted by sex-mad kids only able to manage a couple of quick thrusts and climaxing before she had even begun to enjoy it.

Annie had taken to wearing loose floppy black jumpers, bits of large beady necklaces joined together, patched jeans and sandals. She contemplated a bit of body piercing but decided that the hassle she would get at home when her mother found out wasn't worth it.

Last Saturday, she had gone to a party in a friend's house. The main objective for everyone there had been, as usual, to drink to the point where they could just about stay conscious enough to have sex before collapsing. Annie had met one of the others on the same college course there, a stringy fellow in weird clothes who called himself, Jonah. "Something to do with his feeling for whales," or so he told Annie. Annie had often noticed him but never really spoken to him, he always seemed as if he were on a different planet. But he was so different to anyone Annie had ever met at home that she become quite fascinated. He had sat there drinking only apple juice, dreamily smoking what looked like a bonfire to Annie. "Hi," he had said, "wanna try?" and offered her the joint. "Great," she said, and took her first ever drag. Like everyone who tries a smoke, the first few drags are quite unpleasant. It really is just like holding a bonfire to your face.

Then the effect kicked in.

It was fantastic. Annie floated up and away from reality, just the sort of sensation she had always craved. "Jonah, are you floating like me?" She had sighed, although she wasn't really sure if he or anyone else was with her in her new bright world of colour and feeling. She didn't care either, she was alone and high. Everything was bright, brilliant and shining. Golden colours, dazzling greens, shafts of purple, blues, and every hue was blinding and intense. She saw friends through the mist; she loved everyone and everyone thought she was a queen. Up into the sky she went to a brightness and heat like a sun. She looked down and saw she was naked; her body was just as perfect as she had always known. Skin smooth as silk. Breasts like melons with strawberry nipples. Her centre soft as down. This was the gift she had always wanted to give, to exchange for perfect satisfaction. She felt his hands caress her breasts, her nipples and her very centre. She felt him slip right into her, smooth, long, wonderful, into her very depths. "God, this was paradise!", she heard herself moan as she watched from above and felt him fill her. She was completely and utterly fulfilled.

Sexy, shagged, and for the first time ever, satisfied. She felt Jonah shake her gently; she was in his small room alongside the canal. Never had she woken to such feelings of complete ecstasy. The night had been fantastic, marvellous, brilliant, sexy, exciting and dangerous. Everything she had craved since she was about fourteen years old, and back home living with Mum and Dad.

Since the news of ZENDUST had broken at the New York press conference, her dad, John Douglas, had been on an endless round of meetings, TV interviews, and flights to God knows where. He was everywhere but at home. That Leya woman from DARC always seemed to be with him as well. She had even sometimes answered the phone when Annie had tried to call her dad in some far-off hotel. Annie used to get on well with her dad; he was always much more liberal and understanding of her adventures into boyfriends, parties, late nights, sexy tops, and all the other things with which she experimented. Quite a contrast to her mum, Val, who was always nagging her. With Dad away so much, it had become a nightmare living alone with Mum, no fun, no freedom.

Thank God I got here to college, she thought hazily as she drifted back to the real world. *Here I am now, fucked silly, high as a kite, and free.*

"Are you OK?"

She heard as if from a long way away.

"I'm fine, really fine, absolutely great," she responded to Jonah's worried voice. He knew she hadn't done any kind of drugs before and he didn't want any trouble. "Christ," she moaned, "that was fucking marvellous, especially the fucking," as she came back to earth gently and happily.

Jonah touched her hand briefly, "That's great, I just wanted to be sure you were OK," he said as he got up and started to dress. "I've got to go now; make yourself some coffee," came his voice a few minutes later as the door closed behind him.

As Annie gradually came out of the haze of stimulation, her only thought was *I've got to get some more of that stuff.* Bigger, better and more powerful fixes were definitely on her agenda, and as soon as possible. *After all,* she mused, *Dad has the cure to all this stuff so there is really no danger. Nobody knows about ZENDUST or that he is my dad; what a great time I can have!"*

That same night she went down to the back of the station where she knew she could get what she now craved. It was so easy, a couple of brief conversations, a few notes exchanged, and back she went with the small paper packet in her pocket. It seemed a lot of money for such a small packet, but anything is worth a try, she thought to herself. She popped the pills in the solitude of her own room, and promptly passed out of this world into another of incredible colours, sensations, consciousness and brilliance. Her mind whirled around in a new and fantastic dimension, unlike anything she had experienced, better than sex, better than the smoke by far.

It's bloody awful waking up to real life after the fix, was her first thought some hours and days later. Next thing, she was missing all the lectures at college as she spent more time, and all her money, on every kind of fix she could get hold of. It was amazing how quickly the all-consuming habit took hold of Annie's entire life. She didn't care how she got the money, or what she did, the next fix was an absolute essential. There was no other choice. Just like all the others, she had been captured by the next-fix need.

Her tutor called her to see him urgently, she had failed in the term exams, and her work had gone from average to zero in no time at all.

"Annie, we are very concerned about your progress here. We know it sometimes difficult for new students as they leave home and enjoy the freedoms that this college offers, but you are here for a purpose, not a holiday from responsibility."

Annie could scarcely focus on her tutor's face; he was a grey-haired academic who thought of nothing but the intellectual vagaries of English authors. She was only just coming off her latest high and she felt rather pleased she had actually made it to the college today. Still, she realised she would have to be careful, she was having a marvellous time and didn't want to get thrown out of college and have to return home, to Dad, and even worse, Mum.

"I'm sorry, Professor Davies," she whispered through her dry and cracked lips, something she had noticed as an after-effect of the various pills she took. "I haven't been well and I have asked to see the doctor."

The white-haired and kindly academic looked carefully at her, noting her rather vacant eyes, the dilated pupils, and her listless demeanour. He had seen it before, he knew what was going on, and he knew she was on drugs. *What an absolute nightmare these illegal drugs are now,* he thought to himself, *all these young and bright students getting sucked in without realising the consequences.*

"I think you should certainly see the doctor immediately," he said in a quiet but forceful way. "You must know, Annie, that if you carry on with what you are doing, you will end up on the streets, or in jail, or dead." His eyes bored deeply into hers.

He knew, she suddenly realised. He knew of her habit. Her all-consuming need for another fix.

But he didn't know about ZENDUST, and Dad.

Annie dreamed on, oblivious to the warning words coming out of the moving mouth in front of her... they didn't apply to her... she wasn't captured by the habit...

she was free… she could stop… Dad would fix it… she wouldn't be like the others… she could get ZENDUST… life was going to turn out fine…

Chapter 3
Carlo's Offer

DARC's phone systems had been blocked for days after the press conference. The computers clogged with e-mails and letters arrived by the truckload. The media had gone mad with coverage of the ZENDUST announcements — the clips of addicts revitalised and happy were shown endlessly around the world. Frantic personal callers besieged DARC's small office in New Jersey by every possible means. Many had sons and daughters, even parents and friends, exactly like the video clips John had shown of his trial group before ZENDUST. They knew that death or salvation for their loved ones was imminent.

They needed ZENDUST right now, today. Not tomorrow, not next week or month, right now. The Drug Enforcement Agency in the USA and similar organisations throughout the world saw ZENDUST as a salvation for them. All the anti-drug campaigns such as 'Just say no' had failed miserably.

Even Luke Simons, Chairman of SGB, the biggest and richest pharmaceuticals company in the world, had been on the phone and wanted to meet Kent and

Solomons. Companies like SGB didn't take no for an answer, and DARC certainly could not afford to make enemies of SGB with their present need for cash to crank-up ZENDUST production.

The phone rang again in Kent's office.

"Kent," he responded.

"Good morning, Mr Kent, John Douglas here."

"Hi there, John, are you in Sydney now?"

"Just landed and I hope the pick-up is there for me," said Douglas.

"It's all arranged; the rep from Australian TV will be there. Hope you are feeling OK for the media schedule tonight?"

"OK, thanks," Douglas replied, "but I am getting pretty tired of all this media stuff now and I haven't been home to Val since the New York press conference."

"OK, OK, I know how you feel, John, but we have the tiger by the tail and all those addicts out there need to put pressure on their authorities to get ZENDUST approved for use without too much pissing about on even more long-term trials. Doing all this media stuff is keeping the pressure on and, by the way, boosting the value of your DARC stock options. You're gonna be a rich man soon, John, and a media star! Call me and let me know how the show goes," and with that Kent dropped the phone back on the hook. He was getting sick of Douglas complaining.

The big jet taxied to the air-bridge in Sydney. Douglas was first off the plane and getting used to first class treatment now. Passing through baggage pick-up, he was pleasantly surprised when the TV rep turned out to be a lithe and suntanned blonde dressed in an open-necked loose shirt and tight pants. She was a stunner in fact. Douglas really missed Leya's friendly company as she had been assigned back to DARC USA and he hadn't been back home for weeks now. An attractive girl was just what he needed to lift his jet lag, he thought to himself.

"Hi, Dr Douglas. My name is Zoelle and I have been assigned to you for your stay," she smiled.

"Sounds promising," he replied, with an equally friendly smile.

"We have the limo waiting and I will then take you to your hotel and wait while you freshen up for the show tonight. You are on around nine thirty but we have some network interviews scheduled as soon as you are ready."

For a moment Douglas thought she had said 'as soon as he was *randy*'! By God, he had been feeling that way for weeks!!" Life had become a whirl through the world; he had hardly had time to get back home for what seemed like ages and he was missing the intimacy of home and Val. He collected himself. *More of the same, then*, thought Douglas, knowing exactly what questions would be asked and knowing the answers would be the same that he had given on almost every evening news show since New York. *Still at least Zoelle will make the time pass nicely.*

Back in DARC, Kent called Luke Simons of SGB. He had already been given the private line number so that was a very good sign, thought Kent.

"Luke Simons," came the voice down the line. This was indeed big stuff for DARC, usually they were the ones pleading to get a response from big pharma. The boot was on the other foot now with ZENDUST.

"Hi there, Mr Simons, Kent here from DARC."

"Oh hi," replied Simons, "it's great to get your call. You must know that SGB can accelerate the progress of ZENDUST if we work together. We have all the contacts and influence you'll need to get ZENDUST into the markets of the world and we were very impressed with your guy Douglas at the press conference. I'm going to be in the Cayman Islands where we have our world headquarters next week. I'll send the Lear for you and Solomons. Let's talk business and then we can have your man Douglas meet with our people."

"That's just perfect for us too, Mr Simons, let us know the schedule and we'll be there," replied Kent, feeling good.

Luke Simons went on "You must, however, understand this before our meeting, Mr Kent. We at SGB are a very, very powerful company and we will not stand by and let a business opportunity like this ZENDUST thing pass us by. We will be a part of this business with you at DARC or without you. Let's hope we can work things out together."

The phone went dead and left Kent feeling less than good. SGB were big sharks and DARC were minnows swimming in the same water. The next morning, SGB's intentions were made quite clear in the *Wall Street Journal*. *"SGB announces that they are meeting DARC next week to discuss the commercialisation of their innovative new anti-drug addiction treatment ZENDUST. SGB wishes to reach an agreement to assist DARC in meeting the urgent needs of drug addicts worldwide for a cure such as ZENDUST. SGB would like to emphasise that this potentially important breakthrough in drug treatment is part of SGB's future plans with or without DARC's association."*

The next morning, SGB's Wall Street share price had shot up $5 per share and DARC's had fallen back, much to Solomons' anger. Cursing SGB and Simons, he calculated that he was $370 million poorer as a result, and he was not a happy man. At DARC's board meeting on the day following, Kent and Solomons discussed the SGB announcement and their own weakness compared with the commercial clout of SGB. Douglas was not at the meeting. He was, after all, just an employee and all his work belonged to DARC.

Solomons quickly pointed out, "SGB's offer is OK but our business is to maximise our value to existing shareholders, specifically all of us sitting around this table, not to benefit bastards like SGB. How are we going to do that? SGB are big sharks and we are little fish. We'll meet them next week as they want but we will keep our cards close. Douglas will not go. He is doing a great job for DARC by shunting around the world telling everyone how great ZENDUST is and keeping DARC's share price on the move!"

"We have two options: go with SGB or some other pharm-giant, where we will get screwed as soon as Douglas has opened his mouth and told them what to do, or, option two, find an investor to give DARC the means to do it ourselves. But this is big, big dollars. Who has that kind of dough available and is willing to let us in DARC do it without them interfering too much?"

"Only the guys from Colombia selling all this hard-drug cocaine and other crap already, they have billions they are trying to launder and don't know what to do with!!!! laughed Kent.

However, many a true word is spoken in jest, because at that same moment, Carlo and Juan, his father, were sitting in their beautiful country mansion talking about ZENDUST. Juan favoured the approach that had served him well over the years: get the guy's wife and children, explain clearly to Douglas what will happen to them, in good detail, send him an ear or finger or some other token to help him make up his mind, or just kill the guy. Maybe just torch the place. Firebombs and chopped-off body parts had usually helped folk to see things as Juan Carioli wanted.

Simple, thought Juan Carioli, but Carlo lived in a different world to that of his father. The Carioli family business was now enormous and included many legitimate operations. They had hotels, casinos, discos and clubs all over the world as well as investments in ready cash. After all, the illegal drug business was in cash, and they had plenty of it. Carlo had realised early on that life was different now for the business. It wasn't for him to go round beating up suppliers, terrorising competitors, killing their wives and children or chopping off fingers, ears, or other bits to help people make up their minds the Carioli way. He had plenty of heavyweight thugs around to do that for him as necessary, and sometimes it was indeed necessary.

He had been to Harvard Business School and had learned the tools of trade that the Carioli business needed now. He dressed in dark suits, white button-down collared shirts and looked—and indeed was, the successful modern corporate man. His olive complexion and black flashing eyes, his muscular and lean body, his hard 'don't question me' demeanour, and his money brought him every luxury or woman he fancied. He looked at problems like ZENDUST as he would have any other Harvard exercise.

"I'm thinking of you, Carlo," said Juan. "We cannot simply let the drug business die; it is our lifeblood for everything. He must be stopped."

"I know, Father," replied Carlo, "but this ZENDUST thing has already gone too far for us to kill it by simply dealing with Douglas. Firebombing DARC or whacking Douglas would not mean the end of ZENDUST. It is in every newspaper and he keeps on

44

going around the world talking about it every day. It looks unstoppable. It's a problem. We need to find some way to deal with it. Some new way. Not chopping up his kids or bumping him off. In fact, it would make things worse as there would be a massive campaign on TV and in the newspapers to come after people like us and the other families in the trade. We have to be smarter than that."

Carlo turned away and poured himself another whisky from the silver flagon on the glass table, set by the window which looked out across the beautiful garden that was his father's pride and joy.

We cannot lose all this, he thought. He banged the glass down on the table.

"Douglas! What a pain in the ass he is. Why couldn't he keep his nose out of things? It wasn't as if he or his kids were crackheads. Think, Carlo, think!!"

Fire bombings, mutilations and murder had their part to play in the cocaine business, he knew that very well. But this was different. This was a business problem. What would my Professor at Harvard thought of, he mused?

For years, their main business problem had been that they amassed so much money, mostly in cash, from their cocaine and crack business that they were always looking to go legitimate and invest in legal businesses. It had often been quite a problem. They needed something big. They had billions in cash dollars on their hands and readily available.

"This ZENDUST might kill our business. Using our cash wouldn't be a problem if that happened, we just wouldn't have any cash! Use your head, Carlo, there must be a way forward."

Juan carried on drinking whisky and thinking it out until he fell asleep. In the morning, he woke up with a hangover but felt good. Inspiration and a solution had come into his head overnight. Thank Christ., he thought, remembering for a moment his catholic upbringing and his need for divine help . What a good job I went to Harvard Business School!!

"This is gonna be brilliant. If you can't beat them, then join them."

Overnight and overcome with fine whisky, he had realised that the Carioli family had millions of dollars burning holes in numbered accounts all over the place and he had connected with what he read about DARC's need for massive funds to commercialise ZENDUST. "If the illegal crack and cocaine business was on the way out, where better to be invested than in the business that would replace it?"

This was good Harvard-thinking, business replacement. *We should invest in ZENDUST,* he concluded. That's the answer, everyone's a winner. DARC, ourselves and the other cocaine families

The idea was great, but he needed to think long and hard about the approach he would take in the next phone call he had to make. It had to sound plausible. He had to have a story to tell that he knew his listener would want to hear.

Harvard would be proud of me, he thought, *it might even be one of their classical case studies in years to come.* He smiled at the thought and picked up the phone to call Solomons at DARC.

"Mr Solomons," he said smoothly, "my name is Carlo Carioli and I represent investors with significant resources. We feel that ZENDUST will be a great boon to the world. We are ethical investors and ZENDUST exactly fits the projects in which we take an interest. We know that you would like to go forward independently without the stifling control of a company such as SGB, a company we know that is not always as pure and ethical in their business practices as those in which we take an interest. We can fund your ZENDUST project and bring the benefits to the world as quickly as possible. With that in mind, I would like to know, could we meet?"

This was like manna from heaven to Solomon's ears. "Why, sure thing," he replied, raising his eyes to heaven in thanksgiving to whatever god had sent him this present. "I will be in touch then," said Carioli, and the phone went dead.

Solomons realised that he hadn't even got a return call number or any details at all about these mysterious ethical investors.

"What the hell," he smiled to himself, "this looks good to me. If this guy delivers, then we are in business. SGB can go fuck themselves."

For Carlo, there was another lesson he had learnt at Harvard: keep all your options open and explore all possibilities.

Smiling to himself he thought, *These guys at DARC would shit themselves if they knew where the money was coming from, still, that's their problem.*

Thinking more about exploring all possibilities, he said to himself, "Maybe the old ways of my father should not be completely forgotten, there may come a time when we will need the old ways. We don't know how things will turn out but we do know how to deal with difficult people and problems.." With that he called out to his secretary, "Would you get Diego for me?"

Diego was an old friend of Carlo's and they had shared many a good time together. He was a handsome, black-haired guy who could make friends easily. Especially with women.

"Diego," said Carlo as the call connected, "I want you get to know the family of this guy Douglas who has this ZENDUST stuff. Learn about his daughter, what she likes, what turns her on, anything that might be useful to us. And his wife too, she might be feeling lonely as Douglas keeps going round the world."

"How close would you like me to get to them?" asked Diego.

"As close as you fancy. Be friendly; nothing else," was the instruction, at which there was a knowing smile from Diego.

He knew his job; he had done this many times before when the Carioli family wanted someone to see things their way. Diego set off for England the very next day. He knew very well that when Carlo said, 'Do this job', it was wise to obey.

He was lithe and well-muscled, and always well dressed. He knew very well how to make himself agreeable to women of whatever age, depending on what Carlo told him to do. His face was clean-shaven, but with a small scar across his cheek under his right eye. Women were always intrigued as to how he acquired this scar. He had stories to suit all listeners. Manipulation of the female sex was his stock-in-trade. His deep-set black eyes could change from laughing and friendly to a powerful menace in a flash. This chameleon-like change from friend to foe was also part of his range. He was only of average height, which was helpful. He didn't like to dominate or intimidate the women to whom he was assigned. At least, not until it became necessary.

It was easy to locate the Douglas' home. Diego rented an apartment nearby in a good residential area, well-furnished and tastefully appointed; a place where he could invite back women like Douglas' wife or his daughter, depending on how things went. They would feel comfortable there, not embarrassed or threatened, just as he wanted.

Carlo was satisfied. Diego was on his way to see to Douglas' wife and family as needed. *If the new way doesn't work, then the old methods are still there,* he thought. He was happy too with his offer to DARC, his offers were rarely refused.

For the moment he could smile and relax.

Chapter 4
Lives change with ZENDUST

John Douglas was having the time of his life. Everywhere he went, he was greeted as a saviour. One day he would be in Melbourne, the next on his way to somewhere like Tokyo. He hadn't seen so many cities, so many first-class hotels, so many first-class check-ins at airports in the whole of his life. Every airport welcomed him; he well remembered the many times when he had sat at the back of the plane, squashed into an economy class seat and envied those able to sit up at the front in first class. Now it was, *'Good evening, Dr Douglas, welcome to (whatever) airlines, would you care to wait in the lounge and I will call you when we are ready for boarding? Would you care for a drink whilst you are waiting?'* Not only that, on arrival at every stop-off, he had the most attractive 'meeters and greeters' he could have imagined to welcome him and make sure he had every comfort that he needed, or indeed fancied.

He was evolving into a media star. The constant grooming for TV appearances had made his hair glossier and his complexion softer, without any of the lines that had begun to grow when he was a reclusive scientist away from the bright lights. When there was a break, he would often relax on a beach or by the pool of some luxury hotel where he happened to be staying. His body tan was also coming along nicely, he thought. He had come to realise the importance of being savvy and looking good for the media. And they couldn't get enough of him!! Now he was appearing in late-night chat shows as well as the normal round of meetings with healthcare officials, drug control agencies, addiction clinics and DARC press conferences.

He had, unusually, he thought, become a target for predatory women; a new and slightly exciting feeling.

"It must be their power complex," he said to himself, and turned his thoughts to how things were back home. He did not take up any of the invitations from good-looking women eager to share his bed, tempting though they often were. He thought of his work and Val back home. He called home as often as possible but the time zones didn't always help and he knew Val hated the phone going in the middle of the night.

All these cities and countries he visited had drug problems. The curse of drug addiction had penetrated every country on the globe and nowhere was there a solution in sight until ZENDUST had appeared on the scene. Drug addiction was a pernicious and killing disease that was the root cause of petty crime in communities up and down every land. All these thousands of addicts were trapped into the all-encompassing need for their next fix by cocaine and crack coming out of countries like Colombia and supplied by families such as the Cariolis. They were the living dead of hardcore addicts and a source of criminality; they terrorised neighbourhoods and caused social problems that threatened to overwhelm all that any state could offer in the way of help and medical treatment. They all needed money every day to feed their habits. Not every other day, every day. And they used whatever means they had to get it: murder, theft, prostitution, muggings, anything to get their daily fix.

These addicts, their countries, their families and their neighbourhoods all needed what Douglas had in ZENDUST, quickly and badly. John Douglas was delivering what they all craved and they loved him. ZENDUST had certainly changed Douglas' life and he was loving every minute of it.

Back home in Birmingham, life was also changing for Val. John was hardly ever there nowadays. When he did manage to fit in a visit home, it was a nightmare. The TV and press camped outside and they were besieged. The phone would ring constantly. There were endless demands on John's time when he was at home. She had often been asked to appear on shows with him, write articles about him and their home life, or the woman's perspective of what a benefit ZENDUST will be to young girls. She had always declined. It wasn't her thing at all.

In the circumstances, their sex life had become practically non-existent. He was always busy, or tired, or out. That was it. And that was the way it was likely to be for ever, Val thought to herself. She missed her lovemaking with John. She had tried hard to keep John interested when he had been home and had sometimes put on the black silk nightdress that he had brought her from Paris and lain on the bed letting her breasts fall out of the low-cut top. She was still only thirty-seven years old, and she had kept herself in good shape, especially her full breasts and upturned nipples, which John had always enjoyed caressing and kissing in their foreplay. But it hadn't worked.

Sometimes, quite often in fact, she wished all this ZENDUST furore had never happened. Val's ZENDUST was not what she wanted.

Thank God I have the boutique, she thought more and more. But even that had become a bit of a problem. Half the people who came in didn't want to buy, they wanted to talk about ZENDUST and their own kids who were always on the edge of trouble. Even her partner in the business was beginning to realise Val was a problem at the shop and it was beginning to look as though it would be better if Val left it entirely.

Not only that, but Annie had gone away to college and Val didn't often hear from her.

"Oh well," she said to herself, "I suppose all kids are like that when they get away to college," but the house was so quiet without them both.

54

Whenever she met her old friends for coffee or round at the supermarket, all she ever heard was: "Isn't John wonderful?" "You must be delighted for him," "Fancy John being on that late-night chat show. We stayed up, especially to see him!". Nobody asked how she was, or how she felt. It was John, John, John, even from her own friends. She seemed to have ceased to exist. She was no longer Val; she was that famous John Douglas' wife.

She had given up helping at the local drop-in drug clinic. Since the news of ZENDUST had hit the headlines, every time she went to the clinic, she was faced with desperate cases who wanted to know when the treatment would become available and every last detail, none of which she knew. It was John's work, not hers. She couldn't tell them, help them, or answer anything at all about ZENDUST. She felt helpless and useless at the clinic, so she stopped going to help out.

Another strand of her life was falling to bits. She had good friends amongst the volunteers and staff at the clinic and she missed it a lot. It had been the one thing she had been able to do which was connected with John's work but even that had now disappeared.

The house had become too quiet for her too. She was on her own for much of the time because John was always travelling and she felt vulnerable. In bed, alone, at night, she missed being able to turn over, cuddle up and share those moments of intimacy. When she got up in the mornings and took her shower, she often caught sight of herself in the mirror. She was still slim and good-looking, with long golden-coloured hair, not so different from when she had married John she liked to think. They'd had Annie very quickly and Val had been assiduous in getting back into shape after the birth. She knew John had enjoyed their lovemaking in the quiet of their bedroom at home. Outside he liked to show her off when they attended some conference or other; he had always had an eye for a good looker but there had never been anyone but Val for John Douglas. Now he was hardly ever home and Val missed her man constantly. John had suggested she get a dog for company and peace of mind when the house was quiet and they had gone off together to the local dog's home. It was about the only thing they had done together for what seemed weeks.

This then was Val's changed life. ZENDUST had done this to her. There were now gaps whereas before there had been none. So Rags had come into her life and filled a gap. Val lavished all her redundant love on this great, hairy, ragged mongrel of a dog who, in turn, seemed to love her, was delighted when she returned from the shops, knocked everything flying when the doorbell went and barked at anything that seemed to threaten her. She took Rags for regular walks in the nearby park. It wasn't so much taking Rags for a walk, she often thought, it was more a case of letting Rags off the lead, watching him disappear out of sight and then finding a comfy bench to sit on and wait patiently for his return. But she loved the fresh air and the thought that in the park at least, no one would come up and start on about the marvellous John and what a great thing ZENDUST would be.

Her ZENDUST experience was not great so far. *Quite the opposite in fact*, she thought.

Occasionally, as she sat there and watched the world go by, she noticed a black-haired, South American-looking fellow who also strolled through the park. He was always very well dressed, usually in an expensive leather jacket and designer jeans. He had smiled and politely said "Good morning" to her one day as they passed on their separate ways. Val immediately noticed those lovely, deep-set black eyes. She felt a secret tremor run through her. This was the first man to have noticed her for ages. Unconsciously, her step quickened and lightened.

"Don't be silly," she said to herself, "he is about ten years younger than you!"

Nonetheless, she looked forward to her walk with Rags the next day, thinking *perhaps he might be here again.*

Val was completely unaware that Diego was watching her every move.

For Annie, Val's daughter, ZENDUST had created a safe route to a lifestyle revolution. . Annie now experienced an amazing and novel sense of freedom and liberty. She had quickly realised that with ZENDUST and with her dad being the discoverer, she had a safety net to enable her to do any drug she fancied, as many times as she fancied. ZENDUST and Dad would always be there as a backstop if things got out of hand, as they surely would. ZENDUST liberated Annie from any qualms or fears she might have had before. Her dad had said it on TV endlessly, in fact, she could quote his words by heart: "As a result of the study, I was able to determine that the need for the next fix was not entirely a function of the pleasurable effect of the individual drug. There was some common element that stimulated a need for the next fix. My next step was to isolate this element that I have called 'the next fix need component'. If that could be isolated, an inverse action chemical might be possible, and 'next fix need' would become a thing of the past. In other words, we would overcome addiction. There would be no devastating and uncontrollable urge for the next fix. This results in freedom from the urge, the need and the addiction. This desperate urge disappears. This is the key to ZENDUST. Freedom from addiction."

Annie was bright enough to realise the implications of what her dad kept saying. Now she could do anything. Every hit that was going, or available, she was free to try them all. As she saw things, instead of ZENDUST being salvation for the already hooked, and imminently dead, it was the door to a life of no danger from trying any drug that was going. "You can escape from the addiction." That was the message that Dad was telling everyone whenever he was on TV. He preached resurrection and escape from addiction to a normal no-drug lifestyle.

Annie saw it differently. ZENDUST was the key to drugs without danger. Wonderful! This was liberation from danger and an opportunity to try anything. Annie could, she now thought, set about exploiting this liberation with unmitigated enthusiasm. She was young and reasonably pretty, she had a good body and Dad was surely going to make loads of money. The best thing for Annie was that she had a direct route to ZENDUST if anything went wrong. She could do anything. Or take anything. Or inject anything. For a start, she thought, if Dad was going to be wealthy there was no point in her trying to get qualifications or job opportunities. The next day she had woken up knowing that today's lecture was on 'Poetry and Philosophy in the 17th Century'.

Oh my God, she thought to herself, *there has got to be more to life than this*, so she packed a bag, ignored all those books on subjects that were not of the remotest interest to her and left that world behind. She never even bothered to say goodbye to any of her college mates. *Let them get on with their tedious little lives,* she thought. *I've got a different life to go for.*

The only person who noticed her absence from class was the gaunt and emaciated Jonah, who had shared his smoke with her. He wondered where she was, for he had really liked Annie.

"Perhaps we will meet again someplace, sometime, somewhere," he was sure he had heard those words before, maybe in one of his trances, or hazy drug-induced dreams.

Her tutor, who had seen the onset of her drug addiction, and did not know that the famous Dr Douglas was her father, could do nothing except write to her family and let them know that Annie Douglas appeared to have terminated her course.

What a waste, he had thought as he had written his letter. *So many bright young talents fall to this curse. They come here to college, full of life and expectation, start on alcohol, then hash, then God knows what and then they are on the slippery slope to crime, muggings, burglaries, prostitution and all too often an early death by overdose in some backstreet dump. What a dreadful waste. I truly wish that Dr Douglas well in his efforts to eliminate this dreadful drug addiction problem. God help him and all those young kids like Annie.*

Annie set about exploiting her liberated life. This was going to be her Zen-like karma.

Chapter 5
DARC takes to Carlo

Carlo had, as he promised, spoken to Solomons a couple of days after his initial call and invited him and Kent to a meeting in order to set out his ideas for a partnership between DARC and Carlo's ethical investor group.

"Come out to the Cayman Islands," invited Carlo. "This is where we operate, as we have large investments and new funds available, the supervisory business regime here is accommodating to our requirements."

"Why not," agreed Solomons. "It would certainly be a damn sight better than the drive into Manhattan."

"Please be at Newark's Business Jet Centre for ten a.m. on Tuesday, and I will meet you here on arrival," said Carlo.

"The man and the meeting were living up to our hopes, at least so far," said Solomons to Kent as he replaced the phone. They flew down from Newark in a rented Lear jet, very discreet and low-key. They would quickly learn that Carlo Carioli did not go in for spendthrift ostentation. A black Mercedes sedan waited for them and took them out into the sunshine of the Caymans. In a few minutes, they pulled into the rear of a small, modern and suitably discreet office block. The driver, who had not spoken to Kent or Solomons, showed them to a black-panelled door, in the South American style, with a brass and highly polished nameplate announcing, 'JC Investments'. This was the only bit of ostentation that Carlo had approved, it was his father's name, 'Juan Carioli Investments'.

An efficient and mature secretary was waiting for them and immediately led them into a spacious but spartan office, with a large desk, a leather recliner, and a set of black matching leather sofas around a glass coffee-style table. There was only one picture on the walls. It seemed to be a religious painting, a cross and weeping women, with angels in the background although neither Kent nor Solomons was well versed in religious artefacts. Perhaps this guy Carioli was a Catholic, they thought.

Carlo Carioli came immediately forward and greeted them with the usual banalities of business meetings, "Would you care for some coffee? Was the flight satisfactory? Very pleased that they could come, and so on."

They seated themselves around the glass table, Kent and Solomons independently taking in their surroundings,

Just like a banker's office, went through both of their minds.

Carlo opened up the meeting by saying, "As I outlined in my original telephone call, I represent a group of ethical investors with substantial funds available. We read every day of the terrible effects on our young people and on government budgets of the awful trade in addictive drugs, especially those like cocaine and crack from which there seems to be no escape. Until now, it appears, with your Dr John Douglas and ZENDUST."

In fact, Carlo and his father had called a meeting of the leading cocaine families a week ago. There were only five families that really counted in the hard-drug business and they were not now competitors. They had been at one time, but the business had grown astronomically and there was room for the five families without the need for more killing of insiders.

Each of the five families was flush with cash and the problem uppermost with all of them was how to launder it. Carlo had outlined his plan to use the cash they had accumulated in the illegal business to invest in what might one day supplant that same illegal business.

"We must invest in ZENDUST," he had said. It was a wonderful example of lateral thinking, as taught by Harvard. The families at the meeting couldn't believe what they were hearing from Carlo. "We cannot ignore ZENDUST" he said, pressing on. "It will not go away, and we can't simply bump off Douglas or kidnap his family. There would be a huge effort to track down the killers or kidnappers of Douglas or his family and we might be traced. That's no good at all, we must think differently. We have mountains of cash between us, and if the cocaine business is dead then what could be better than that we should be involved in the replacement? I propose we should invest in ZENDUST!!"

He talked about the cash they had available, the need to legalise their businesses as much as possible and to see their own children being able to walk freely in the legitimate business world without the stigma of association with illegal drugs. A lot of the sense of what Carlo had said came through to the families as they listened very carefully. These were hard-headed business people now, not street-corner pushers, and this was a business strategy for the future. Like a corporate plan for the biggest illegal business in the world.

What a good thing I sent Carlo to Harvard Business School, thought his father.

They had eventually all agreed that ZENDUST was potentially such a problem to their business that although the idea of investing directly in ZENDUST was not what they really wanted, it was perhaps the only way out. If coke and crack were on the way out and ZENDUST was next, then so be it. Carlo had secured his investor group with ready money in the billions of dollars.

As the meeting broke up, Francisco Gomez, patriarch of the Gomez cocaine business, had looked Carlo and his father in the eyes and said, "This had better work. This idea of getting involved with ZENDUST. I and my family have a very good business now and we feed many, addicts who want what we supply, with big profits to us. If there are problems in the future with your plan," — emphasising the word 'your' — "I and my family will do whatever is necessary to keep our business going using any means we can," he repeated. "Including eliminating people who are a threat to me, my family and our business, and that might mean this character Douglas, or his family or even you and your family if you stand in my way. That might look like a return to the bad old days to you, Carlo Carioli, but those methods have worked well for me and for my family for many years. We will be watching you closely to see how things go and we will take action if things seem to be going wrong.

"We will not see our money lost in your new scheme if things go badly. We will do whatever is best for our family." Gomez stared coldly at Carlo, embraced his father for a few moments, paused to let his words sink in, then turned away as his driver opened the door of his car, got into the back seat and drove away without looking back

Carlo had his agreement. He could do what he wanted and none of the families would stand in his way. If Gomez became a problem there were always the old ways. DARC did not need to know that the dollars would come directly from the cocaine business, and from the very same addicts who were suffering the curse that ZENDUST was designed to eradicate. Cocaine and crack and addicts would now fund the solution. This was the reality of JC's ethical investment funds…

Solomons and Kent listened intently as Carlo continued blandly. "We see this as an excellent chance for our group to do some good in the world with the funds we have available. We are business investors, we know that your company, DARC, needs funds to accelerate the ZENDUST work, to build up production, and to build sales worldwide. We have these funds. We also know that companies like yours operate better independently. We believe that if DARC was absorbed into a monolith like the giant SGB Pharmaceuticals, then they may choose to feed ZENDUST to the market in a slower way and hence keep up the price. We do not want to see that happen. We want ZENDUST to meet the needs of addicts worldwide without delay. In fact, we want ZENDUST to be as successful as the illegal drugs business itself is today." Carlo smiled inwardly to himself as he pronounced these words.

"In addition, speaking as one businessman to you two businessmen who have kindly come here today, we know that you need your own rewards. We therefore propose that DARC should remain wholly in your hands and that you will therefore benefit from the share price and equity options to which we think you are quite rightly entitled. We will take a percentage license fee from the sales of ZENDUST that our injection of funds has permitted. We will take the money in the form of shares in DARC Inc. Our group does not require additional cash reserves. Please be aware that our investors are private people and we do not wish for any publicity regarding the good works we undertake, such as our interest in ZENDUST. That is the reason that you may not have been aware of our existence until today's meeting. We keep a low profile in our ethical investments.

"We do, however, have one important condition. Dr John Douglas must be retained within DARC. He must not be lost to a competitor. We require monthly reports from DARC detailing all the movements and activities of Dr Douglas. He is your prize asset and we wish to be sure that he is looked after in every way possible. We do not mind if he was to be reassigned part-time to an organisation like the UN since we feel that their prestige and involvement can only accelerate the acceptance and hence sales of ZENDUST worldwide. "But we need to know as much about Dr Douglas as possible. That is our proposal."

He smiled at them both, took up his coffee, sat back in his chair and let his words sink into the minds of Solomons and Kent. He knew it was an offer that they would not ignore. Impassive in his innermost and secret thoughts, he knew that his Harvard Business School professor would have been proud of his performance that morning. All of it was attractive to DARC, he knew that; all of it proclaimed their interest in doing good to the world; all of it meant that Kent and Solomons would be rich men, and all of it was solely in the interest of JC Investments. If the cocaine and crack business was really on the way out, then JC Investments were well placed for the future with this proposed involvement with ZENDUST.

Solomons looked once at his colleague and replied, "Thank you very much indeed Mr Carioli for your clear presentation. We respect and admire your desire to use your funds in the interests of young people worldwide with this addiction affliction. Naturally, we must discuss your offer within our company before we can make a definitive response.

"However, I have to tell you right now that what you and your investment group propose is of the greatest interest to me, Mr Kent, and, I am sure, all of us in DARC including Dr Douglas. We hope that such collaboration with your investors could lead to ZENDUST becoming the most successful drug the world has ever seen."

With that, there was little more to say and the car was ordered to take the two DARC representatives back to the airport. Carlo personally saw them both to the door and into the waiting car, shaking hands with each of them, and wishing them a pleasant journey back to Newark. He watched them go and smiled contentedly to himself. They were well and truly hooked, he knew from experience. It was an offer they couldn't possibly refuse.

As they got into the limousine, behind the soundproof glass which screened them from their taciturn driver, Kent and Solomons looked at each other in delight.

"That was a breeze, what a prospect, money from them, we get rich as DARC's stock market value shoots up, and they don't interfere. What could be better!!!"

They were ecstatic. No need to talk to SGB, or anyone else. As they flew back to Newark and enjoyed the champagne hospitality that Carlo had made sure was available for their return, Kent and Solomons laughed and joked.

"Did you see the nameplate on their door," laughed Solomons. "JC Investments. Does that really mean Jesus Christ Investments!!! It must be, did you see that picture on the wall? What a joke that would be! ZENDUST, as funded by Jesus Christ!"

They enjoyed their ride home that night.

Immediately they left the offices of JC Investments, the side door into Carlo's office opened. His father, the Juan Carioli whose initials were on the brass plate outside, entered and clasped his son in his arms, kissing him on both cheeks in the South American way. He had watched and listened to every minute of the DARC meeting via the secret TV camera that monitored every meeting held in that office.

"You did well, my son. Perhaps you are right, the old ways are past and your new ways are the future. Without your training, education, intelligence, and your ability to think of solutions that I could never have imagined, we may have been ruined. I am so proud of you."

Juan was not normally an emotional person; he had learnt in the past to be able to shoot a man dead without a second thought if that was necessary. Now he realised that he was getting on in years, the time had come to hand over to his son and go back to a peaceful and pleasant time with his wife of many years in their beautiful garden in Medellín. He embraced his son for a few more long minutes. There were tears in his eyes. "Call the car please Carlo, I will go back home now."

Carlo was now the man in charge. The new ways were now the right ways. At least as far as he could see at the moment. Nonetheless, he would call Diego tomorrow and see if he was getting close to Douglas' wife. And he must locate the daughter Annie as soon as possible. *There might yet be a place for the old ways,* he thought, *you never know what might happen.* He was right in that thought, too.

For now, he had his solution to the ZENDUST problem. Within days, DARC had called Carlo and accepted their proposal. Things happened quickly enough from thereon. The cash flowed into DARC as Carlo Carioli and JC Investments had promised. ZENDUST was gearing up for major international trials and approvals. As Carlo had predicted, the UN had taken an interest in this worldwide issue that affected so many of its member states. They offered to sponsor the trials of ZENDUST with Dr John Douglas as their major international ambassador. They established the UN

ZENDUST Anti-Addiction Programme which became known as UNZAP.

John Douglas was now more famous on the planet than Jesus Christ, as John Lennon of the Beatles had once famously said of that band. DARC was making money and their share price on Wall Street was zooming upward. Carlo and Juan were happy. Their drugs cash was now funding the anti-drug business. This was Harvard's theory of Business Renewal at its best.

Maybe I will become an Honorary Professor someday!! thought Carlo.

Chapter 6
ZENDUST Takes Off

The boost given by the international UNZAP Programme and the cash from JC Investments kickstarted the growth of ZENDUST. DARC could barely keep up with the flow of demands for trials in various countries. Addicts and their families couldn't wait to get in touch with DARC. The UN was particularly delighted with their UNZAP Action Programme, after all the debacles they had been involved with in recent years in places like Iraq, Lebanon and Israel, not to mention the various scandals and accusations of mismanagement and corruption within. Here was a big chance to do some good and to be seen to be helping to solve one of the world's worst and endemic problems, hard-drug addiction and all the associated crime that fed the habit that eventually killed the users. The UN Secretary-General had lunch with John Douglas and the press was once again there to record the event and help to rebuild the organisation's reputation for being a force for good.

DARC was cranking up production of ZENDUST as fast as they possibly could. New staff had been hired and all other research programmes had been dumped in the rush to meet the demand. They had never experienced anything like, nor ever would again, thought Solomons. In that thought, he was to be proved correct by subsequent events in the life of ZENDUST. As far as Kent and Solomons were concerned, there was absolutely no need to waste funds on any other research work. ZENDUST was going to make them so much money they couldn't give a damn about what might come next.

They were delighted too with the UNZAP Programme which had enabled DARC to short-circuit some of the very demanding, tedious and expensive procedures that any new pharmaceutical product had to satisfy for approval for use worldwide. UNZAP were keen on ZENDUST and were putting in place an approvals regime which would bring ZENDUST to the world markets without delay. They responded to the criticisms of this procedure, especially by rival pharmaceutical companies such as SGB, by pointing out the massive queues for ZENDUST at clinics worldwide.

Luke Simons, CEO of SGB, mentally cursed DARC and UNZAP roundly as he sat at his monthly board meeting. Ever since the original press conference for ZENDUST, he had been pursued by his company's shareholders wanting to know what he was going to do about either getting an agreement with DARC or developing their own competitor product.

"A ZENDUST clone is what SGB urgently needs" said his bankers and investors, who had billions committed to SGB, and were at the meeting.

"I have previously told you about the offer we made to DARC," he repeated angrily, although he knew very well he would do himself no favours in publicly correcting powerful board members of SGB. "We are aware that DARC has attracted major investment funds which have enabled them to move forward aggressively. They therefore turned down our offer; indeed, Solomons, their CEO, did not even bother to return my call. We do not know the source of their funds but it's obviously substantial and a closely kept secret otherwise we would have found out from our contacts in the investment banks, isn't that true, Joe? Furthermore, the UNZAP Programme has given them a fast track to markets worldwide. It is quite unprecedented. We are therefore committing our own funds to developing our ZENDUST clone and it is top priority in our research facilities. We will be in this ZENDUST market, with or without John Douglas or DARC." Privately, Simons fully intended to drive DARC out of business; he was not used to being upstaged by runts like DARC or encountering people who didn't return calls from him, the boss of one of the biggest pharmaceutical companies in the world.

"There are queues for this product at drug clinics throughout the world," noted Joe Goldstein, one of the senior SGB board members and chairman of his Wall

Street Investment Banking Corporation, who had been with SGB for many years. "We cannot be caught out this time as we were with the Viagra business. We were late to market then and never fully caught up."

"It will not happen," Simons assured them. "We will not just have a clone, ours will be better than ZENDUST. Have confidence in our company's power and resources.

"There is another very important point for us to remember in this rush for ZENDUST. Rushing new pharmaceuticals to market sometimes causes tremendous problems when things don't work out as everyone expects. Remember the thalidomide disaster and all those deformed births. That kind of scandal might kill us as a company. If ZENDUST gets used by millions of consumers, as it will, and then there are problems, who knows what the unexpected effects might be."

Simon's last remark turned out to be the prediction of the century. ZENDUST was to have a life that no one would ever have predicted. Goldstein was right about the queues: the first were the seriously hooked addicts, just like all the test cases that Douglas had shown in the videos released after the now famous press conference. They and their families were desperate to get ZENDUST before, inevitably, death put a stop to their addictions, followed by the consequent tragic cremations of family members, sons, and daughters.

They were exactly the tragic cases on which Douglas had focused all of his work. He had always had in his mind a messianic zeal to do some good to the world. His work on ZENDUST had given him that opportunity. To him, it was heaven-sent. He always looked back to a friend he had met in his first week at university. His name was David, and he had been a real soulmate for John; they had done everything together to join in university life. They were both single children of parents who loved them almost to excess. These two babies, boys, teenagers, and now young men had been the complete focus of the lives of each set of parents, to the exclusion of all else. They had led sheltered lives in the protective nests of loving parents and the release of getting away to university had been like the metamorphosis of a butterfly from the all-enveloping and restrictive pupa. But David had gone out of control within a few weeks of living with this freedom. He couldn't handle it. Within six months, he was dead from an overdose, and the life of the best friend he had ever had, John Douglas, was snuffed out. He had been totally devastated by the experience.

He had resolved that he would dedicate his life to trying to make sure the same thing never happened again. Good young people killed by drug abuse.

He had no time now to reflect on the similarity between his dead friend David's life and that of his own daughter Annie. He was so busy. He remembered that Val had told him that a letter had come from the college saying Anne had apparently given up her course but they had received a letter from Anne a day or two later saying she had left because the course did not suit her. Neither letter mentioned the drug problem that was the real cause of Anne leaving. Anne said she was going to visit some friends and would write again soon.

So that seems to be fine, thought John as he was waiting for a plane to take him onwards to New York. *She must be OK and we will wait to hear from her.* Thinking that Anne was going to turn out OK was to become the biggest mistake of his life.

He was totally engrossed in his work. He was thrilled by the sight of all these sad, desperate, emaciated, imminently dead addicts now putting a stop to their deadly compulsions for their next fix by coming into his programme, and turning to the opportunity that ZENDUST had created.

As the availability of ZENDUST spread internationally under the UNZAP Programme, the beneficial knock-on effects were such as to heap yet more praise and adulation on his head. It was turning into a reversal of all the evil effects that highly addictive illegal drugs had caused. Petty crime and burglaries dropped as addicts turned to new lives. Addiction clinics, once overloaded, were becoming surplus; healthcare costs were dropping; needle infections were becoming a thing of the past; deaths by overdose were dropping fast.

Best of all, in the mind of Dr John Douglas, were the pictures of families reunited with their sons and daughters, once lost to addiction, now returned to life. For them, ZENDUST had lived up to the promise of a peaceful karma that its name had offered.

He was an international superstar, he didn't have enough time to think about his own family.

Chapter 7
Diego and Val and Anne

Val had a new interest in her life. Every morning she woke up showered, dressed well and looked forward to taking Rags for his walk. Every morning now she met up with the charming young man with the flashing black eyes, and they walked and talked. He had said "Good morning" to her a few weeks ago and stopped to stroke Rags. He said he was a language student and was in England for three months to learn to speak English. He always walked in the morning and he wondered if he might walk with Val and talk to her in order to practise his English.

She had been rather thrilled at the chance to talk to such a pleasant and rather good-looking young man, it seemed harmless enough to walk and talk together as they walked in the park. She hadn't had anyone to talk to, let alone a rather attractive and exotic-looking young man, for some time. When John did phone her, it never seemed to be a very satisfactory call, he was always due off for another meeting or she had just come in from the shops and they never really talked to each other as they had done in the old days. Then they would often have gone out for lunch at some delightful country pub, enjoyed a bottle of wine and discussed all manner of things. That did not happen any more.

A few weeks ago, Carlo had called Diego and told him that John Douglas seemed to be all over the world and never at home.

"Listen to me, Diego," Carlo had said. "His wife Val might be feeling lonely and neglected and might be receptive to some of your South American charm."

It had always helped before if the Caroli business had a hold over the target of their interest and to have Diego close to or preferably in bed with Mrs John Douglas might prove to be very useful as time went by.

"Get close" was the message from Carlo. After this call, Diego ensured he met her every morning. He noticed how she was looking much more attractive now than the first few times he had seen her. He didn't realise that she had noticed him just as much as he had kept a close eye on her.

Every morning he said, "Hello and how are you? I hope it will be a sunny day."

She had got used to him speaking to her and began to welcome it. She often didn't talk to anyone else all day.

"Your English is coming along very well," she usually said, and then talked about the weather, as the English always do.

Diego would then always stroke the dog, Rags, and say something like, "You must need to walk a long way every day to tire Rags out. I like walking in the mornings too and I have a dog at home," to put Val at her ease, although he never said where his home actually was. He was a smooth operator and Carlo had given him his instructions. The Douglas family was very important to Carlo's plans, and Diego intended to get close. Val was, after all, quite attractive and Diego had not got involved with any women since Carlo had told him to come to England.

I wonder what she would be like in bed had crossed his mind several times.

Val always felt at ease talking to anyone when she had Rags with her. Rags was a big strong mongrel and she was confident that if there was any trouble then he would soon bark and growl. Diego realised that he needed to be sure that Rags saw him as a friend and not a threat.

That day, Val had not slept well because of her worries about Annie. It was like that frequently at night now, worries and loneliness, and no one to talk to. "I know she wrote to say why she was giving up the college course, but we haven't heard from her since. I wonder if she is okay," she said to herself as she set off for her morning walk. It was a bright and sunny day and she was looking forward to meeting the South American lad with the attractive dark flashing eyes with whom she had struck up a friendship. *Perhaps I might mention my concerns to him; he was a student too and he might also have friends who knew Annie,* she thought to herself.

He was there, as usual. He always wore that black leather jacket which made him seem rather like one of those singers she had innocently lusted after when she had been a younger.

"Good morning" she said brightly.

"Hello, and you are looking very attractive today," replied Diego.

"Don't tease me," she said, although she was secretly delighted at the flattering and rather intimate comments that Diego made when they met.

"It is a lovely day, is it not?" said Diego.

"Your English is coming along very well," replied Val as usual, "but I have a few family problems on my mind so I haven't really noticed the lovely sunshine this morning."

"You looked so well; I cannot believe you have problems."

"Families are often difficult," said Val. "My daughter has left college and I don't really know where she is or where she has gone. She is only eighteen and of course, I am a bit worried. Her dad, my husband, works away a lot so I don't really know what to do. I shouldn't really be saying this to you anyway, but it helps to talk."

Val had no idea that Diego knew exactly every detail of her life and of the absence of her famous husband, the great Dr John Douglas. Carlo had been getting the monthly reports from DARC with every last detail of Douglas' lifestyle, travel and evening entertainments, and very interesting they had been too. There was more to Douglas than met the eye, Diego knew, and far more than he had ever told his wife, Val.

"Please, talk on, we have a nice day for a walk and I have no class today so to hear you talk is very helpful for me," replied Diego.

"I am so worried about my daughter, Annie," she said, "so worried. She hasn't written for weeks now; she isn't like that; she was always so close to me before she went away to college. I really don't know what to do and my husband John isn't here to help. I am alone and cannot seem to do anything except wonder where on earth she is. I wonder if she has got into trouble with the police, but that would be so unlike her. It could be a boyfriend or, even worse, an older man. She was always on the lookout for older boys and we had to talk to her a lot about not getting too involved or even pregnant. I'd hate to think she has gone off and was having sex with some awful man she hardly knows. Even that would be better than if she has got involved with drugs, God forbid. That would be absolutely awful. You don't know anything about our family, so you cannot possibly know how terrible that would be."

Her pent-up emotions were overwhelming her as the words tumbled out. It was such an enormous relief for her to talk and suddenly she could not control her feelings, she suddenly let go, and lost control as the tears welled up in her eyes. Feeling weak at the knees, she almost collapsed. Diego quickly put an arm around her to stop her falling to the ground.

"Perhaps you should go home," he suggested. "I will walk with you; it will be fine."

"Oh, thank you so much," she said wiping her eyes as the tears were now freely flowing. This was a release of all the emotions that she had been holding tightly together since Anne's last letter.

She walked home in a dream and a confusion of tears and relief at having let go of her feelings. Diego led her inside. Val looked for the comfort of his warm and strong arms and he held her tight. No one had held her like that for months

This is so lovely, she thought, enjoying the closeness of a man for the first time for ages. Feeling him against her body, her mouth found his and as she looked deeply into those dark black flashing eyes, she kissed him hungrily.

Diego knew she was ready. He had been told to get close to Val by Carlo and this was the opportunity. She needed and wanted him at that moment. She needed no encouragement. He took her upstairs and laid her gently on the bed. He stripped off his clothes. She felt so wanton, so free, so eager for love, so wanting a man. She raised her body so that he could easily remove her blouse and her bra. She lifted her legs so that he could ease her skirt and panties down over her ankles. She lay there naked, exposed and expectant, with all her needs for loving and caring dominating her every fibre. He let her see his muscular hard body as he moved around the bed and she noticed specially his olive-coloured skin and the two small round scars on his left shoulder. He lay beside her, kissing her, caressing her and loving her. She had never felt the need for loving as much as she did at that moment. Her breasts responded to his hands and mouth in a way they had never done with John. Her nipples were erect, her body moist and she was completely ready as he slipped into her. She let him love her freely with no restraint. Her body tingled from top to toe, from nipple to nipple, to thighs and legs and in between. Long, deep and hard he loved her. She came with all the ecstatic thrill of an orgasm such as she had never experienced in all her life. She cried out, fell limp, and buried her head in his warm strong arms.

Waking, she wondered what she had done. This wasn't like her at all; she wasn't a woman to fall into bed with anyone, but she was satisfied, contented and replete at that moment. She slipped out of the bed and put on the silk dressing gown that John had bought for her in Japan.

Diego stirred, smiled at her, and said, "You were wonderful."

Val felt a momentary depth of happiness that she had not felt for a long time but she knew that it was the worry of Anne that had brought things to a head this morning and resulted in her finding herself naked and satisfied by this young man Diego.

"Please understand me," she said, looking at this young man lying in her bed with his bare chest and two odd-looking scars on his shoulder, "I told you that I am so worried about my daughter and my loneliness and worries got the better of me. I am not one of your easy lays. In fact, I have never done it with anyone else but my husband. But he's always away nowadays and I am so alone. There is no one I know that I can talk to or might help me. Whatever has happened to my daughter, and where she is... it's on my mind every minute of every day. I just don't know what to do," she held her head in her hands and tears started again.

He stood up beside her and held her again, telling her "Please listen to me. I have many friends. I can help you find her. Do not worry."

She sat down on the side of the bed, trying to stop crying, hoping desperately that what Diego said might be true.

He lifted her head in his hands and looked deep into her eyes, "I say again, do not worry; we will find Annie for you. I have many powerful friends."

With that, he left Val sitting on the side of the bed, dressed quickly, kissed her briefly on the cheek saying, "Don't worry, I and my friends will help," and went out through the front door, closing it gently behind him.

Oh God Val thought. *If only he can.*

As the door shut, she collapsed back onto the bed. Val had such a fantastic whirl of emotions going in her head at that moment. She had been made love to, and it had been wonderful, by a young man she hardly knew. Now he had said he would find Annie, and he had powerful friends. Whatever did that mean? He hadn't said but had talked as if there was absolutely no doubt that he or his friends would indeed find Annie. She had wanted sex and had lain naked and exposed, to a virtual stranger, all the things she had warned her daughter not to do. She remembered the two little round scars on his shoulder, were they possibly bullet wounds…? She had let him do things to her… who was he…?

My God, I really don't know anything about him at all. What have I done? she thought to herself, in a mixture of tears, satiated sexual desire, desperate anxiety about Annie and hope that Diego would do what he said. Or his powerful friends would. Whoever they were.

Diego called Carlo as soon as he was back in his apartment. Carlo knew what to do. The hunt for Annie was on the very next day.

Val sat, wept and hoped.

Chapter 8
Annie gets hooked

Annie was spending half of her days stoned out of her mind and the other half looking for her next fix and the money to feed the habit. Since leaving that boring college, she had gone on a spree of abandonment. She had not even told her friend Jonah that she was going, just packed and left. She tried everything she get hold of smokes, pills, drinks but nothing satisfied now. She needed it mainline, in the arm.

It had been OK on the soft stuff when she had been with Jonah, but after a few of them it was boring, no kick. He had been nice to her though, they'd had great sex together and she often thought fondly of him in her sober moments, which weren't very many these days.

Jonah had never known about her dad, the famous Dr John Douglas.

Jonah had always stuck to the smokes, he had told Annie, "You will be OK with this stuff, no real problems, everyone does them, no bad effects. I stay off anything else, too dangerous. I don't want to end up as a junkie on the street."

Annie had just smiled as he said this. She knew she was as free as a bird to get anything, try anything, inject anything: ZENDUST would be there for her when she wanted. Straight from Dad. A lifeline. For the present, Annie was out for the big time. For Annie, ZENDUST was a key to the door of being able to try anything, with no real danger. ZENDUST was her key to do whatever she wanted. *Good old Dad, he has really done me a good turn with ZENDUST, he wouldn't ever realise it though!*

Today was one of her better days, she had been able to get some money from a guy at the drop-in charity, after she told him she was hungry and needed a bed for the night.

"Don't just go off and get another fix," he had said, "just get some food and a rest. You look awful."

These charity guys are fools, Annie had thought. *What does he think I am, crazy? Well, yes, I am crazy actually, I'm crazy to get something to give me a lift and, for sure, food isn't it.*

Round at the back of the station was where she usually went for her supplies, but that was getting difficult for her now. Sometimes she didn't have the cash and they had learnt not to give any stash without getting the cash in hand. "No cash, no stash" was the message. Annie went into the ladies' loo and had a look in the mirror.

"Oh my God," she said to herself, "what a bloody awful sight."

The charity guy was at least right there in what he had said, she *was* a mess. She got out her comb and pulled it through her hair, straightened her jumper and pulled it tight around her body. *Still got nice tits*, she thought, as she looked herself over. Straightening her clothes, she pulled herself together; she didn't like anyone to say she looked awful. She still had a bit of pride in her good looks.

All the money that Dad and Mum had given her for college had run out a few weeks ago. She needed the next fix; the urge was getting more and more irresistible every time. More and more desperate. But the highs were just as good too, the problem was they just didn't last as long. *I need something with more kick*, she thought. *That's the answer.* She never bothered to think that the treadmill she was on was exactly the same treadmill that her father was talking about every day at ZENDUST press conferences. *I can stop when I am ready*, was Annie's answer in her head. *I am not hooked, I'm not a crazy junkie.*

She went round to her dealer, a big dark-haired powerful-looking guy with flashy rings on his fingers, and a black leather coat. In the dark, sometimes you could only see his rings shining gaudily under the street lights but he didn't like that joke.

"That stuff I had yesterday, it was no good. Didn't last five minutes. I've got a bit of money, here look. But I want some good stuff or give me my money back."

He immediately grabbed her by both arms and slapped her hard on the face, "Don't you try to fuck about with me. You got some cash? No? That's not enough. So, get some more or fuck off!!"

Annie fell back as he shoved her away; she was pleading, almost crying.

"I'll get some cash, later, just give me some stuff to get me going again. Now. I really need it."

"You heard! Go get some cash. Go and knock off someone's house, pinch some old lady's handbag, go on the game, whatever. That's your problem. That's it. No cash, no stash."

He turned away, got into his car, slammed the door and drove off.

She fell back against the wall of the station. A few of the girls on the game had been watching her, knowing what was going on. The back of the station was well-known as the place for punters to get a hooker or find a dealer.

Annie was feeling terrible now. She needed the next fix desperately. She must get some money somehow; she knew that was the only way. She sat down on the wall next to the toilets, holding her head in her hands, in a terrible state.

I must get some decent cash. Now, not tomorrow or next week. I need it now. The thought was irresistible. *But how?* She sat for several minutes, getting herself together, thinking a bit more straight now after the shoving around from the dealer. As she sat there, a guy in a Jaguar stopped in front of her. He looked her up and down, noticed her good figure, let down the car window and said, "You free?"

At first, Annie didn't really know what was going on, why did he say that she wondered?" Then she realised, *He thinks I'm on the game!!*

"Hey, you, are you free? I'm busy and there are plenty of girls here," he called out.

She thought for no more than a millisecond. *Here is a guy ready to give me the cash I need, a quick fuck and I can get what I want. Why not? I've fucked plenty of guys for free, why not get some cash?*

She jumped up, leaned into the car window, giving him an eyeful of her big tits, and said, "Yes, a quick one though, in the car."

She needed the cash and the fix quickly; she had no time for an all-night session. Opening the car door, she jumped in and the car shot off. The police often took numbers of the punters and he didn't need that kind of hassle.

She felt across his lap and massaged his crotch as he drove round to the wooded area near the golf course.

The sooner he comes, the better, thought Annie, as she felt him respond. He stopped the car, turned towards her and started to feel her breasts.

"No; money first," said Annie pulling down her jumper. He took out his wallet, peeled off the notes and Annie put them into her pocket.

Great, she thought. *Easy as pie.*

A few minutes later, it was all over. He pulled up his zipper, said nothing, started the car and drove back towards the station. Annie jumped out of the car, ran round the back of the station and sure enough, her dealer was back.

"You got the cash?" he said abruptly.

"Sure have," replied Annie. "You got something good this time?"

"I have everything you need," he smiled knowingly. "How did you get the cash, fuck someone?"

"Just give me the stuff," said Annie as she handed over all the cash she had got, a few minutes ago. She felt a bit soiled and damp between the legs, but so what, she had what she wanted, needed, craved, so desperately. Back home, she got the kit together, burnt the line, chased the dragon and got the high she had needed.

Next day though, it was all over. The high was gone, back to reality: unsettled, hungry but couldn't eat, very thirsty, itching all over, pains coming and overwhelming her, then going away for a few moments. But she knew that another line of crack would solve the problem. Still no money, but now she knew how to get it. Easy as pie. The dealer said she could have the stuff she wanted if she would work for him. "Most of the girls round here are mine," he said.

"Will you give me the stuff now?"

"OK, but you'll owe me," said the big black-haired guy, smiling at her. Within a week, she was fucking as many guys as he brought to her. Sometimes five or even ten a night.

The fixes were always there, every night; she was hooked. There was now no escape. Fucking for fixes. That was her life. She had forgotten about Dad, Mum, her life; even her thoughts that drugs were something she could give up easily, especially with Dad's ZENDUST.

Annie was a hooker, and totally hooked.

Chapter 9
Finding Annie

Diego was on the hunt. Carlo called him practically every day wanting to know if he had made any progress. Diego had stopped walking in the park after the time he had been with Val but he had called her and said he would be away for a while and that he was searching for Annie, as he had promised.

Diego went down to the college where Val had told him Annie had gone. It was easy for him to go into the student area, buy some drinks and talk to people who had known Annie.

"She just up and offed one day," they told him.

"What about any boyfriend, did she have anyone special?" he asked.

"I think she knew a guy called Jonah," one of her friends said, "but he was never at the college so we didn't know him really. She used to go down to the BlackBone Club to meet him, but it's a dive and there are lots of druggies there. The college has banned us from going there, too much trouble. We told her not to get involved, but she was always one to do her own thing."

"Thanks a lot," said Diego. It was a start.

In Medellín, the families had met again and talked about ZENDUST and their usual drug businesses. They were worried, ZENDUST was OK but it didn't bring in the cash like cocaine did.

Fernando Gomez had made it clear "Things have to get better; we are losing money from the crack and cocaine business and ZENDUST just don't look like bringing in the same kind of money. What are you gonna do?" he said, looking at Carlo.

"Give it time," said Carlo, "you would be losing more if we weren't in the ZENDUST business at the same time as the crack and coke stuff."

"Well, it ain't good enough for me and my family," rasped Gomez, "We may have to get a hold on the business ourselves. Not leave everything to the Carioli family," and with that he had walked out, with his brothers his son, Rico, and Rico's young son, Santiago. As the Gomez family got into their car, Fernando called Rico over, telling him "Get on a plane and go to England. Get Douglas' wife or daughter. The daughter, that'd be best and bring her back here. We need to put some pressure on this guy to get a deal about the crack and this ZENDUST. Don't tell Carioli what you are doing, just find her and bring her here."

The very next day, Rico landed at Heathrow, passed quickly through customs and called a taxi. He had been told where Douglas lived and told the driver to take him straight there. "Wait," he told the driver, and he went up and knocked on the door. Val was delighted when she looked out and saw a man standing there who looked exactly like Diego. She rushed to the door "Are you a friend of Diego's?" she asked. "Have you found my Annie? Come in and tell me the news!"

Rico was astonished, he hadn't expected anything like this. As he went in, he thought quickly, and realised that the Cariolis were after Annie too.

"We haven't found her yet, but I need you to tell me a few more things," said Rico. Val thought it was a bit strange, when this new fellow seemed not to know all the things she had told Diego, but they certainly seemed very keen to find Annie, so that was great.

She repeated all the story about how Annie had given up college that she had told Diego, and asked Rico, "How was Diego? Is he down at Annie's college now finding out where she is?"

"Sure is," said Rico, I'm just going down to help him right now. I'll get him to call you as soon as I can."

"Oh, thank you so much. And thank Diego as well, when you meet him, I can't wait to find out where Annie is and if she is OK."

Rico got up and said, "I've got to go now and see what we can do to bring Annie home as soon as I can. I have a taxi waiting outside. I'll call you," and with that he walked out of the door and left Val in a state of great euphoria.

He must be one of the powerful friends that Diego had mentioned, she thought to herself. *Thank God I have someone to help my Annie.*

It never occurred to her that when this man Rico had said 'I'll bring Annie home as soon as I can', he had meant his home in Medellín, Colombia, South America, not the cosy little Douglas home in Birmingham.

Rico couldn't believe his luck. Instead of having to work on the wife, she had told him everything he wanted. Not only that, but he also now knew that the Cariolis wanted to get their hands on Annie too. His father would value that important bit of information. His father was a hard and very demanding taskmaster, as Rico had learnt over the years. He thought to himself, *I'll call him on the mobile now, he will want to know what's going on and what the Cariolis are doing behind our backs.* He dialled home, shutting the glass between himself and the taxi-driver to stop the driver from eavesdropping.

His father was furious at what Rico told him. "Maybe this ZENDUST thing is a scam to get control of the cocaine business for themselves, those bastard Cariolis, especially that smart-arse kid, Carlo. One thing's for sure, Rico, you had better get to the daughter first. I can just see old father Cariolis face when I tell him who we have hidden away. Carlo's plan will go to hell, and good riddance…" the phone in Rico's hand went dead suddenly.

Rico knew his father very well. When he said you had better get to the daughter first, he really meant it. God help Rico if Carlo Carioli got to Annie before him, he didn't fancy confronting his father with that kind of bad news. Still, the mother, Val, had given him a great start. The race for Annie was on.

Rico told the taxi driver to take him to the car-hire centre, he needed his own wheels. He set off immediately in the black Mercedes coupe that he had hired for cash. He knew where Annie's college was, he had been to England many times before and knew his way around.

The students in the bar were quite bemused to have another South American asking the same questions that they had answered a day ago. Rico took in all that they said, bought them a beer and went directly to the BlackBone Club. He parked the Merc outside the door, looked around to try to be sure that there were no kids ready to steal his wheels, went in and asked the barman directly, "Was there anyone here called Jonah? I need to contact him about his girlfriend, Annie."

Various blank faces turned towards him. Rico could tell immediately that these were all on the hash or junk. "Anyone here called Jonah?" he repeated loudly.

A bearded, thin, pale and spotty young guy asked back, "Are you the same guy who came here yesterday asking the same question?"

Rico thought on his feet. "Yes," he replied. "Are you Jonah?"

"Yes."

"Can you come out to the car so we can talk?"

Jonah followed Rico out to the car.

"Wow, this is a great motor. Annie must have met some good rich guy!"

They drove out to a quiet spot by the seafront. Rico told the story about how they thought Annie was in big trouble and he needed to find Annie urgently. Jonah had a soft spot for Annie, and that was why he had gone to the BlackBone Club that day. They had told him a South American-looking guy was asking about Annie and he had said he would be back that day to meet him. Jonah told Rico he thought Annie was into the hard stuff and was likely to be in Brighton, probably at the back of the station where everyone knew you could get whatever you wanted.

"I'm OK with hash and smokes. Annie wanted more. Better kicks. Not for me. But I did like Annie and I will look for her myself. I'd like to see her again," said Jonah.

Rico wanted Jonah out of the way for a few days so he felt in his pocket and handed over some of the good hash he usually brought with him to England.

"Thanks a lot. I'll let you know about Annie. Go home and try this stuff, it'll keep you high for days!"

Just to make sure he didn't go back to the BlackBone Club, Rico drove Jonah to his flat and saw him inside. "Try that stuff now," he urged, "and so long!"

Jonah sat down, rolled a tube and moved happily into never-never land.

Back in the Merc, Rico set course for Brighton station.

Diego went back to the BlackBone Club later that night, hoping to meet Jonah.

"Your pal was here earlier," said the barman. "Jonah's told him what you wanted, now get going. We don't need any trouble here. If Annie's in deep, then that's her problem, nothing to do with this place."

Two big bouncers came over, "Can we help you leave now, sir," they said politely, marched him out the door and shoved him away. "Now fuck off and don't come back."

Diego couldn't understand what was going on. Who had been into the BlackBone that day, before him? What should he do now? He decided to call Carlo.

"Carlo, someone else is looking for Annie, as well as us. They have been to see her mother and now they must be ahead of us." Carlo went very quiet on the other end of the phone. He remembered what the Gomez family had said at the meeting.

"The bastards," he said to himself.

"It must be Gomez; they will screw everything up. Do you have your gun, Diego?" he asked.

"No, but I have my knife, it is better and makes no noise. I know how to use it and I have other things with me. From what I hear, Annie might be a junkie so I have some stuff. Is it Rico who is after her as well as me?" said Diego.

"It must be," replied Carlo. "Get going, Diego, get Annie, that's the priority, then call me. I don't want to hear anything more about Rico Gomez. Ever."

As he put the phone back on the hook, Carlo thought about the Gomez family. They had been a thorn in the side of the Carioli family for many years, he thought to himself as he poured some of the strong black coffee he liked. *If Diego does have to eliminate Rico, then it will lead to a vendetta, I know that, but as it is, old Gomez is a fool if he doesn't come to terms with what is happening. ZENDUST and all that. It had to happen one day. We, the Carioli family, are smart enough to know that. Gomez and his family think only that a few more killings will fix it. If it is to be a vendetta, then so be it.*

Diego knew what Carlo had meant. He went over the things that Annie's friends had said when he had called into the college and at the BlackBone. There had been something about Annie liking Brighton as a place where she could get anything. There was no other clue. He had to start somewhere. He drove fast but carefully; this was no time to be stopped for speeding. Unbeknown to him, he was only a few hours behind Rico.

Rico went straight round to the back of the station, it was only early evening and there was no one about, no girls or dealers. He went into a pub, ordered a beer and sat down in a corner to wait. Val had given him a picture of Annie so he knew exactly who he was looking for, the only thing was, was she a hooker or just a junkie coming here to buy a fix? He decided not to ask any questions; he had no intention of letting anyone remember him. Around ten thirty, he left the pub, and walked around. The girls were out in force now, eyeing him, giving him the come-on, and the dealers were there too. He looked carefully as he passed the girls who looked back and smiled encouragingly. He kept looking for the one he wanted, but there was no sign of her. Perhaps she only came to buy stuff, so he watched the dealers just as carefully as they did the business.

He saw that one of the girls was arguing with a big black-haired dealer, who shoved her away, shouting, "Get back out there and get some punters. When you have the cash, you can get the stash."

She staggered back, shaking all over and weak with the effort of arguing, obviously needing the fix desperately. As she turned away, Rico recognised her immediately. It was Annie Douglas.

He watched her go back to the street, realising that she had to get some punters and some cash before she could get the stash she needed so urgently. Although she couldn't stand all the men she let fuck her, and she was so sore from doing it five or six times a night, it was the only way, and she knew it. She needed to sell herself again, and quick, so she opened her blouse a bit more to let the punters see what they would get and stood directly under the street light. She had to attract a punter as soon as she could to get the cash to feed her desperate urge for the next fix.

Rico watched carefully, and then approached her "You free?" he asked.

She got herself together as best she could, leaned towards him, showing her breasts and smiled openly at him.

A punter, thank God she thought. "Sure I am; you got a car? What's your name?"

"Rico," was the reply. "Over here, it's the black Merc."

She followed Rico back to the big black car, as he turned away to open the door, she saw someone else suddenly emerge out of the shadows and step up behind this guy Rico. There was a flash of something metallic, and he seemed to shove something in Rico's back, and push him headlong into the Merc. Rico collapsed into the car without a sound. His head went down on the steering wheel, and his eyes looked blankly ahead. He didn't move. Didn't even breathe.

Diego quickly shut the door of the Merc, took Annie's arm and said, "Annie, I know who you are; I have talked to your mother. We have been looking for you; we are friends, and we have everything you need. That guy I shoved into the car was only a weirdo punter. Come with me; my name is Diego."

Annie was transfixed. What had happened? Was that other guy dead? Had this Diego killed him in front of her eyes? God, she felt so awful, near to collapse and stunned by all this.

"I, I don't know… I need a fix… do you have some stuff?" She was almost crying with desperation.

Diego smiled at her. "Yes, I have; as I said, we have everything you need. Come with me, I have a car over there."

It was an offer she didn't refuse.

Chapter 10
Euphoria all Round

Dr John Douglas was enjoying the euphoria of the success of his ZENDUST treatment. He was the superstar, feted by everyone for the thousands—nearly millions now, of addicts who had used ZENDUST and were off the treadmill to death. Governments in Europe, the USA and many other countries were feeling the benefits as their costs of policing drug traffickers, drug-related crime, and dealing with addicts at clinics and rehab centres were dropping fast. DARC were as happy as pigs in muck, as the saying went. Sales of ZENDUST were rocketing upwards, tracked by the upwardly mobile share price of DARC on Wall Street.

The only negative was that they had heard that Luke Simons, CEO of SGB Pharmaceuticals, had held a press conference announcing that their version of ZENDUST would be available soon and would, as Simons had announced, "Be better than ZENDUST in every respect."

That announcement had dented the DARC share price somewhat, but DARC's investment backers, JC Investments, seemed contented. DARC had reported back to Mr Carlo Carioli of JC Investments every month. The reports included details of Dr John Douglas' whereabouts, schedule and lifestyle, as Carlo had requested. DARC had thought that was a bit odd, but after all, Douglas was the key to the success of their collaboration with JC Investments, so why shouldn't they want to know what he was doing?

Back home, his wife Val was euphoric after the phone call from Diego telling her he had found Annie and that she was fine. The phone had gone late at night. She had been in a complete tangle of emotions ever since the incident at home with Diego and his talk about being able to find Annie and those mysterious '"powerful friends" he had mentioned. Every minute of waiting had seemed an age. She was so anxious about what had happened with Diego and whether he really could help to find Annie that when the phone actually did ring, she had picked it up very gingerly. She knew it wouldn't be John; he never called late in the evening.

"Mrs Douglas, this is your friend, Diego."

Val's heart was in her mouth. What was he going to say? Was Annie in trouble, dead even; whatever had happened, where was she?" All these questions ran through her mind like an express train. She felt weak at the knees, just as she had when she had first told Diego about her problems. She remembered again what had happened then with Diego at home, upstairs. She sank down in the chair...

"Mrs Douglas, is that you? I have excellent news. I have found Annie and she's fine. She is staying at the apartment of a friend as she has not been well for a week or so. She sends her love to you and her dad and hopes to see you again soon. Everything will be fine, don't worry any more and I will call again in a few days."

The line went dead before Val could respond. There were so many questions unanswered, she wanted to ask where they were? Had she been ill? Had she seen a doctor? Where had she been since she left college… there was such a lot she didn't know.

She had phoned John immediately. He was somewhere in New York. *Goodness knows where,* she thought but she always used his mobile.

"John darling, thank God you answered, great news, Annie's friend phoned to tell us she was fine but had been a bit ill so that's why she hadn't been in touch. I don't know what she had, her friend didn't say, but anyway she is apparently OK and will call again soon. Please come home soon, John, we have such a lot to talk about."

"That's wonderful news, Val, I knew Annie would be all right. We always brought her up to be sensible and keep away from things like drugs and the wrong sort of men."

At that moment, the door of his hotel room opened and in walked his PA for the day, "Dr Douglas, you have the UN meeting in twenty minutes, are you ready?"

"Val, I have to go now, I'll call again as soon as I get a minute. Ask Annie's friend where she is and what she is up to after leaving college; we want to know everything!"

One thing Val certainly didn't know, and Diego did not tell her, was that Annie was a junkie, hooked on drugs, desperate for her next fix. Annie was at that moment floating in her own private euphoria, brought on by the fix that Diego had provided.

Diego couldn't believe it when he had found Annie and discovered what she had become. He had led her back to his car quickly and quietly. They had to get away without any fuss from the black Merc and the dead body of Rico Gomez sprawled over the front seat. He quickly realised that Annie Douglas, the daughter of the Dr John Douglas famous for his work on the cure for hard drug addiction, was herself a junkie and couldn't wait to get her next fix. She was desperate as she had followed Diego to his car.

"You said, you had some stuff! I need it now, can't you see," she was crying pitifully and clinging to him, "please, please give me some."

"I have it in the car, get in."

She almost collapsed as she sagged into the back seat of Diego's car. "Here, use this," and he passed a little white packet back to her. She knew what to do, and within a minute she had passed into never-never land as the effects struck home in her bloodstream. Diego drove swiftly away from scene, and onto the motorway, travelling north out of Brighton. He needed to be well away before any alarm was raised. He aimed for Carlo's London apartment, where he would call Carlo and be able to keep Annie secure for a while.

John was delighted with the way the UN meeting had gone; he came back to the hotel on a high. Everything was going swimmingly! The PA, who said her name was Rose and looked very attractive in her tight white top and dark skirt, had been great; it had all gone exactly to plan and the UNZAP support was being expanded to more countries cursed with the illegal drug addiction problem. John was ecstatic, he didn't want the day to end. As they got back to his hotel, he did something he had never done before with any of the girls who had helped him along his various journeys: he asked Rose if she would care for a drink with him.

"Great, I'd love to," said Rose.

He ordered a large Glenlivet whisky and asked her what she fancied.

"Quite a lot," smiled Rose mischievously, "but to drink I'll have a martini."

John suddenly realised the message she was giving him was 'I'm available'. He got the drink for her and was careful to sit on the other side of the table; thoughts of his wife Val and daughter back home had surfaced in his consciousness. He quickly finished the whisky, without saying much more to Rose. He said, "Thanks a lot for your help today, you were great. Please finish your drink, but I am really bushed and I need to get to bed. Goodnight, see you tomorrow," and he got up abruptly and left her sitting there.

Rose wanted to get to bed too, but with the famous Dr John Douglas. *Oh well, there's always another day. He's got to need to have some sex one day, I just need to be sure I'm around when he does* and with that delicious thought, she finished the drink and went to her room. Alone. At that moment, John was happy to confine his euphoria to his great success with ZENDUST.

In Medellín, Fernando Gomez was brooding over what had happened to his son, Rico. The British police had informed him that Rico had been found stabbed to death in an area renowned for drug abuse and prostitution. The police had assumed that Rico Gomez had been murdered by person or persons unknown in the course of a drug crime or an argument with a pimp. No witnesses had been found. They did not have any leads as to who may have been responsible. They would let him know if any progress was made in finding his killer but at the moment there were no suspects.

Fernando Gomez had other ideas. He knew Rico had been on the trail of the Douglas girl and that one of Carlo Carioli's men had also been on the hunt. "In my heart, I know Rico is dead because of the Cariolis. They will pay the price. There will be more deaths and this time it will be the Carioli family, not the Gomez family. My family will have vengeance." He set his heart on killing Carlo Carioli, the man Carioli had sent to find the Douglas girl in Britain, and the Douglas family who

111

had caused him so much grief as the cocaine business declined with the success of ZENDUST. "Others may be happy with ZENDUST, but I will only be happy when I am avenged on those who have caused the death of my beloved son, Rico. Vengeance will be mine and then I will be content, but not until then. However, I am a patient man, and it will taste all the sweeter when it happens, when Carlo Carioli is dead, preferably at my feet." With that satisfying thought in his head, he sat down by his fireside with a glass of whisky and contemplated the euphoria which would surely come his way, in its own good time.

Chapter 11
Unexpected Outcomes

Carlo was absolutely amazed when Diego called with the news of Annie's addiction. "How do you know that? It can't be! For God's sake she's the daughter of that guy Douglas with all that ZENDUST shit. Are you sure?"

"I picked her up when she was on the game as a hooker to get some cash to give to the dealer who was running her. I had to give her some stuff in the back of the car to calm her down, she was desperate for a fix, all crying, yelling, and shaking, you know what they're like. She was zonked out by the time I got to the apartment and she is still flat out; I had some good stuff with me and she had that. She will probably be out of it for at least another couple of hours. What a fucking unexpected turn-up this is!"

"No kidding," said Carlo. "Give me a while to think this out and I'll call you back. Just make sure she stays with you; don't let her out of your sight. If she needs some more stuff, give her what she wants. We don't want her out looking for a dealer. Have you got plenty?"

"Yes, enough, I'll call you if I need some more. You can talk to your friends in London, they will give us some more crack or whatever she needs."

"OK, take good care of her, she is valuable!" and Carlo put the phone down. To have John Douglas' daughter a junkie, and in his hands, was like manna from heaven, as he remembered the story the priests had told him during his Catholic upbringing. Like all well-brought-up children in Colombia, he had been to a school run by monks and could recite the catechism by heart. He never thought much about that people that had been murdered on his instructions: that was business, not personal.

How did the girl Annie get into such a mess, with all that her father has been doing with ZENDUST? he mused. He never thought about all the nameless millions that his family had entrapped into the hell of drug addiction; in fact, he rarely saw a junkie himself, it was all far removed from the business of growing, refining and shipping the stuff around the world. *I would never let anyone in my family get into such a mess. Diego will have to get her to talk and see what happened and why she did it.*

He picked up the phone again. "Diego, listen to me, when she wakes, be kind to her; give her what she wants, but be sure to talk to her. We need to know why she took to the hard stuff. Most kids don't unless there is some big family trouble or something else. We need to know why she started; it could be useful. Anything at all that we get to know about the Douglas family could be valuable. Use your South American charm on her!"

"It'll be a pleasure," responded Diego. He had seen how Annie had looked under the street lamps when she was trying desperately to get a punter. He smiled to himself and looked at the sleeping body of Annie Douglas in his bed.

He sat and waited. After several hours, Annie stirred, rubbed her eyes, and looked around and then closed her eyes again.

"Whoa, that was some stuff," she said. A few minutes later, her eyes opened again, she looked around, and saw Diego sitting nearby.

"Who the hell are you?" she asked.

"My name is Diego. I'm the guy that took you away from that idiot punter and that dealer who was going to beat you up." Annie thought on this for some minutes, as if coming down from a cloud back to earthly reality.

"I don't remember."

That's good, thought Diego. He didn't want any awkward questions as to what had actually happened that night, and why Rico had suddenly collapsed into his car. Diego had deliberately given Annie a high-strength dose of heroin in the hope that her memory would be obliterated and it seemed to have worked.

"Do you want some coffee?"

Annie was just coming to after the fix. "Yes," she replied, sinking back on the bed. Diego brewed some strong black coffee and gave her a cup. She drank it down; she was always thirsty after a fix.

"You look as though you could do with a shower." Annie was awake now after the strong bitter taste of the coffee. She looked around, and then down at herself: a skimpy blouse open at the front, a short black skirt, no shoes, they must have been lost somewhere.

"Are you a punter?" she asked. "The last thing I remember was that I was out looking for a guy to give me some cash for a fuck. I needed the cash for a fix. Is that what you want, a fuck?"

"No, I am a friend. I have been looking for you. I talked to your mother who is worried stiff about you. She knew you had gone missing and that we might be able to help."

"My *mother*! For God's sake don't tell her I was on the game, she would never recover." She suddenly thought of her father too. "And don't talk to my father either."

"It's OK, they don't know you are here. They only know you are safe." Annie couldn't really grasp what was happening. What was this all about? Who was this guy, who claimed to be her saviour? I need time to think.

"I'll take a shower," she said, needing a bit of time. "Where is it?" Diego showed her to the bathroom, it was quite magnificent. Carlo had fitted out his London pad very luxuriously. She closed the door behind her, sat on the loo, and looked around thinking, *whoever this guy is, he has plenty of money, this set-up must have cost a fortune.*

She stripped off the remnants of her clothes and stepped into the shower. She was heartily sick of going around dressed as a hooker. The hot stinging shower brought her back to her senses. In a way, she was glad not to be in a drug-induced state of oblivion although she knew very well that the delicious feeling of being back in humanity wouldn't last long. The next-fix urge would soon return, it was irresistible and all-consuming. She stood there for quite a while, under the jets, in a blank space full of questions. Of family, drugs, the next fix, why she was here, who was he… it went on and on. Eventually she stepped out, brushed and dried her hair. Wrapping herself in a fluffy white bathrobe, she felt ten times better; her self-esteem was returning; she was in control of herself. She went back to talk to this guy Diego.

"Now," she said, looking into his lovely dark black eyes, "would you kindly tell me what this is all about?" Diego replied, "I met your mother as I live nearby and I often walk in the park in the mornings. She was always there with a big dog. One day, she told me that her daughter had gone missing. She was in a dreadful state worrying about where you were and whether you were in some sort of trouble. Your mother was so worried and you seem to have come from such a nice family, it looked like bit of help wouldn't go amiss. I said I could help and here you are. This apartment belongs to a friend of mine." It was, in fact, a very abbreviated explanation of how Annie came to be in Carlo Carioli's flat; Diego didn't mention that he had been to bed with Annie's mother, or that the real reason she was there was because her father was Dr John Douglas, father of ZENDUST.

Annie was really angry to hear all this about her mother and her dad, especially from a stranger. What else did he know, for God's sake?

"A nice family, you said! It was so boring! I was so suffocated in that family, I had to get out to be free and to do my own thing. I needed to get out and try things for myself, instead of being told what was good for me and who I should go out with. All my friends were out having fun at discos and raves and all I got was, 'You're a sensible girl, you don't want to get involved in that stuff'. I had to escape. There was so much I wanted to try; all my friends had taken stuff and had good times, I wanted to try it too. Anyway, I knew that for me there was no real danger."

"Oh," said Diego, "why was there no danger for you? Lots of kids end up with problems if they start taking hard stuff. Why should you be different?"

Annie pulled the bathrobe closer around herself and thought for a few minutes. *Shall I give the game away? I can actually do anything in the way of hard drugs; I may have a few problems but that's because I have gone overboard. With Dad's ZENDUST, I can do whatever drugs I like, if I take ZENDUST as well, I won't have any of the problems of addiction. Dad has eliminated the next-fix urge, as he keeps telling everyone. I know that, so I can take anything, then take ZENDUST and no problems!*

Annie had no idea that Diego already knew all about ZENDUST.

Diego waited for her. "Well, tell me, why are you so different?"

"Because my dad is Dr John Douglas, the man responsible for the anti-addiction ZENDUST treatment. With that stuff, I can do any drug I like, use ZENDUST at the same time, and I will not get hooked into addiction, just have an endless good time. It'll be just like the morning-after pill to stop you getting pregnant! All the fun and none of the after-effects. That's why I'm different. The trouble was I hadn't got the ZENDUST pills. I know I was in a state when you picked me up last night, but that was because I had gone overboard and not asked Dad for the ZENDUST I needed. He would go mad if I asked him for his treatment. So I was just doing the fixes without the ZENDUST antidote which would have kept me sane and safe."

Diego suddenly realised what had happened. *That was it in a nutshell! That's how Annie became a junkie. ZENDUST was the morning-after pill for a full-on fix! John Douglas will never realise what he has done; he has opened the door for everyone to use whatever they want. I'll have to call Carlo. He will be in seventh*

119

heaven when I tell him all this. Diego's mind was in a whirl at the implications of what Annie had just told him.

Annie carried on, "The trouble is I don't have any of dad's ZENDUST, so I got into a bit of a mess with the stuff I was doing." She was beginning to feel the urge to get another fix; the gnawing pangs were just starting and she knew she wouldn't be able to control them. She pulled the robe tightly around her; she could feel the shivers beginning. She could feel her whole mind and body being taken over and consumed, it didn't take long.

"Are you OK?" asked Diego, watching Annie shake and shiver and twitch. He knew exactly what the problem was and what she needed, craved, actually. "I have some good stuff if you need it."

"Oh God, yes."

Annie greedily took the small white packet and disappeared into the bathroom.

ZENDUST a morning-after pill for hard drugs, you can never tell how things will work out. Sometimes, there are the most unexpected outcomes.

Chapter 12
Dealing with the Unexpected

Diego called Carlo and related all that Annie had told him, especially the bit about ZENDUST being the equivalent of the morning-after pill to counteract a good strong dose of crack cocaine or whatever. No after-effects, no compulsion or next-fix urge, all the things that Dr John Douglas had said about ZENDUST, it all fitted.

"Wow, who'd have thought it! Douglas has not just given the junkies and addicts a release from addiction, he has freed everyone to try whatever they want without the danger of getting hooked. It was the same as when the birth control pill was invented, there was no danger of pregnancy so suddenly everyone was fucking anyone without any risk of unwanted consequences. ZENDUST will do the same for illegal drugs."

The implications were fantastic, especially for Carlo who had a finger in both businesses, the illegal drug supply and the manufacture of ZENDUST.

Carlo decided to call Solomons at DARC.

"I have a feeling demand is going to rocket even more for ZENDUST soon," he said. "Be sure to gear up production quickly."

"We are going full blast at the moment," was the reply, "we have the UNZAP Programme in hand and we are having great success in reducing the number of addicts in all the countries in which we are operating. Why do you think we need to go even faster?"

Solomons and his colleagues at DARC were sitting pretty on top of a phenomenal rise in the DARC share price on Wall Street. He couldn't imagine that there was anything else to jack up the share price even more.

"Just a premonition," replied Carlo, "but do what I say. We don't want to miss out if there is a bigger market than we think." Solomons had no idea what Carlo was talking about, but he knew that the guy talked sense. He would call his production department.

Nonetheless, he wondered what it was that Carlo Carioli knew that he didn't.

The main problem Carlo had now was how to make public the news that the danger of illegal drug addiction was over. Finished. Eliminated. For everyone, new users and addicts alike. Perhaps the problem was to keep the lid on the news for a while so he could plan what to do, in true Harvard Business School fashion. Annie must be kept quiet; she mustn't be allowed to go blabbing her thoughts to anyone.

Once the news got out, he knew there would be an explosion in demand for all the illegal drugs his family had been growing, refining and shipping all over the world for many years. He decided to go back and talk to his father, Juan Carioli, at the family ranch in Medellín.

First of all, he called Diego back, "Hi there, thanks for telling me all that Annie Douglas had told you, especially why she felt free to do whatever fixes she wanted with her dad and ZENDUST behind her. Make sure she doesn't tell the same story to anyone. I repeat, *anyone*. Is she OK?"

"I gave her another fix. She's sleeping it off right now." Carlo thought for a moment. "Take her away somewhere out of circulation, take her to the apartment we have in Cannes. You take her yourself, tell her mother she is going on a holiday with you, but don't say where. Tell her Hawaii or Australia or somewhere that her mother won't expect her to call from. Fly her out on our plane; it's still in England. We don't want any trail left if the cops start to look for her and start to trace commercial airline flights or whatever."

Next was his father.

"Father, we have to talk again. I need your advice. This ZENDUST thing is bigger than we thought; it is not bad news. In fact, it could be the biggest thing that has happened to our business for years. I'll tell you all when we meet. I'll come down tomorrow."

Diego phoned the Carioli aircrew immediately. He had never met them and, in fact, he had never used the Carioli private plane before. Carlo had always kept that to himself. Diego knew that he must get Annie out of

123

the country and into the apartment in France before she woke up and started asking questions again. The crew were at the flat within thirty minutes. They were dressed as paramedics and they laid Annie on a stretcher, took her out to the waiting limo and off to the small private aerodrome where the jet was kept. No one even noticed, it all looked so organised and official. She was loaded onto the plane accompanied by paperwork saying she was a patient on her way to a cancer clinic in Germany. None of the officials bothered to check the details. The plane was in the air and on the way to France within two hours of Carlo's instruction. Annie was still zonked out with the quality of the stuff that she had taken. The aircrew were taciturn and had got on with their jobs quietly and efficiently, without saying much to Diego except to be sure he was comfortable.

Diego picked up the airphone and called Annie's home. The phone rang and rang and then the answerphone cut in.

Great, thought Diego. *Now I don't have to get involved in explaining what's happening.*

"Mrs Douglas, this is your friend Diego. I am calling to tell you that Annie wants to have a few weeks away before she comes home to you and her father. She asked me to take her for a holiday somewhere. She wants somewhere very quiet with no phones or people asking her what she is going to do or things about college and all that. She needs to get herself together, she said. She will write as soon as she can. She sends her love. She will be safe, Mrs Douglas, I will look after her and see she is fine. Take care, Diego."

Val came in from the shops just as the phone disconnected.

"Damn it, I wish I had been here five minutes ago." She clicked back the messages, stood by the phone and listened. She was a bit bemused by what she heard, it all sounded very odd. This mysterious Diego always seemed to be involved with her family, and there was that other friend who had turned up at her house asking about Annie, just the day after she had told Diego everything. They all looked a bit South American. Still, there was no alternative, Annie was apparently safe, and going for a holiday with Diego. At that Val shuddered inside. *Oh my God, Annie might get involved with him now, she mustn't find out that he and I had sex together in my bed. The daughter and the mother, Annie and me, with the same man!* and she sank down into the chair overcome with her private thoughts. She couldn't move for thinking about what had happened and what was likely to happen… on that holiday with that South American, Diego.

After about two hours into the flight, the pilot came back and spoke to Diego "We have instructions to go on to Medellín; Mr Carioli thinks it would be safer for the girl to be there, not in France where she might easily escape from the apartment. We will stop over to refuel and then be on our way. Arrival will be in seven hours."

OK, thought Diego, *it is unusual for Carlo to change his mind but who am I to argue?*

He settled back in the recliner, checked that Annie would be insensible for the duration of the extended flight, and dozed off. He felt a tap on his shoulder.

"Landing now; please fasten your seatbelt. Please also give me any weapon you have in case we have an inspection," said the flight attendant.

"I have nothing," said Diego.

"That's good." Annie was moved over to the jump seat just behind Diego, still comatose. The private jet touched down smoothly and taxied round to a private parking area, where a stretch limo was waiting.

Annie was stretchered down, still unconscious and placed in the back of the limo, followed attentively by Diego, who didn't intend to let her out of his sight until they met up with Carlo. As the car drew away from the plane, the other passenger in the front seat turned around, stared at Annie and Diego, and as he automatically locked the car doors, he took out his revolver and pointed it straight at Diego's face, saying, "You are most welcome in my care; my name is Fernando Gomez. I will look after you and the girl now, not the Carioli family. The plane you came in was mine," he smiled, "not Carioli's, I tapped your phone and I know exactly what you intended to do. Your plane is still in England and your aircrew are temporarily incapacitated. I was very pleased you called the girl's mother, that saved us a problem, now she isn't worried about where her daughter is, at least for a while."

"I want very much to talk to you about what happened to my son, Rico" he intoned with an extreme of malice and venom. "As for the girl, she is valuable to my family, but you are not. You all think that the Gomez family are so dumb. Perhaps you and Carlo and Juan will think again now. We in the Gomez family will not be run out of our business, by the Cariolis or anyone else." He turned back, and as he did so, he raised an armoured partition to separate himself from the rear compartment of the limo.

Annie Douglas and Diego were now prisoners of the Gomez family.

Chapter 13
The Wise Man

Fernando Gomez picked up the phone and called Carlo Carioli.

"I have the girl and your man, Diego."

Carlo had known there was something drastically wrong when his own aircrew had not contacted him on plan. He then found out that they had been drugged and tied securely inside the Carioli plane in England. He guessed that the Gomez family were behind it; there was no one else who would have had the nerve to take on the Carioli family in quite the same way. He had waited to hear from them and now the patriarch of the Gomez family was on the phone.

"Senor Gomez, you should know that the business we are both in will be excellent for your family and for the other leading families. There are new things happening which will make you happy. It would not be wise for you to take any strong action until we have spoken."

"What makes me happy is the thought of obtaining vengeance for the killing of my son Rico in England. I think you know about that. But I am a patient man on that matter. As regards our mutual business interests, I will meet you to hear what you have to say. Make sure it will not disappoint me. You must come here to my ranch. Come alone or with your father. You have my family guarantee that you will not be harmed while you are at my house. My family's honour is the guarantee." Fernando Gomez spoke very quietly, he was not accustomed to raising his voice, but there was a firm trace of intense malice behind his words, just as when he had spoken to Diego and Annie in the car the previous day.

Carlo and his father visited the Gomez ranch the next day. Fernando Gomez met them and in the age-old Spanish custom, greeted Juan Carioli with a kiss on both cheeks. As patriarchs of the families, they had known each other since childhood. He briefly acknowledged Carlo with a look of intense hatred.

"Is the girl OK?" asked Carlo as soon as he arrived.

"Yes, I am not a fool; she will be safe with my family. Be patient, do not be so hasty. We must take time for our discussions," Gomez replied curtly.

They entered the Gomez ranch, which was large and luxuriously appointed. There were several armed guards patrolling the grounds; life was never completely secure in that area of the country. The office from which Fernando Gomez ran his crack and cocaine production and distribution business was oak panelled and furnished with soft black leather chairs around a low, highly polished table. In fact, it was very like the office that Juan Carioli maintained. They had, after all, been in the same business as friends, rivals and sometimes enemies for a very long time.

"I am pleased that you have come here so quickly," began Fernando Gomez, "we have many things to discuss and problems to resolve. I do not like to entertain the possibility of making an enemy of the Carioli family with whom my family has been acquainted for many years."

Juan Carioli replied in equally friendly but direct tones. "Fernando, we respect your family and your need to resolve the unfortunate death of your son Rico. We will help you to find who is responsible. We will discuss that later. The girl is a different matter. She is very important for your present cocaine business and ours. But she is also important for the interests both of our families have in the ZENDUST business. My son, Carlo, will explain."

"Senor Gomez, thank you for allowing us to visit you today.

"As you know, we both have investments in the ZENDUST business operated by the American DARC company. That business is doing well. We are making money for your family and ours from our association with DARC through my father's JC Investments company.

"We know that your concern has been that this investment in DARC and ZENDUST would not bring the same rewards as the cocaine and crack business. My father has the same concerns.

"You and I understand also that ZENDUST might ultimately result in the end of our illegal drug business altogether. This might have been true except for what we have learnt from the experience of the Douglas girl, Annie, who is now in your care.

"The girl left her family home and has become addicted to the illegal drugs which are both of our family's main businesses.

"My man, Diego, has become her friend and she trusts him.

"The girl allowed herself to become an addict because she knew that her father, the great Dr Douglas, would always be able to give her his ZENDUST drug control treatment. For her, therefore, there was never any danger in allowing herself to use any drug she could obtain. Of course, drugs on the streets are expensive as we know and she became a hooker to feed her habit. In fact, she was enjoying the crack and cocaine so much that she became unable or unwilling to ask her father for the ZENDUST treatment.

"The important lesson for your family and ours — and it is the most surprising and satisfactory outcome that we could both have wished for — is that the girl has shown us the way to keep our present business and to continue with our ZENDUST investment.

"We can arrange that it becomes known that ZENDUST can act as a 'morning-after' pill for our mainstream addictive drugs. In this way, our drugs can be used without the dangers of addiction. As Douglas himself keeps saying, ZENDUST overcomes addiction. If that is so, then many more will want to use our drugs knowing that ZENDUST removes the danger.

"This is an excellent outcome for our family businesses. Our sales of crack and cocaine will grow more than ever before when it becomes known that the dangers of addiction are eliminated and that the enjoyable effects of our drugs can be experienced without the dangers that have existed hitherto.

"Of course, we know that it has been the addictive properties of our drugs that have ensured a continuing demand from users. This information from the Douglas girl's experience means that as her news gets out into the media, there will be millions of people worldwide who will now perhaps turn to the drugs we provide because they will be safe. The properties of crack and cocaine that give wonderful highs of experience will also mean that these new users will keep going back for more. The difference now is that these new users will know that ZENDUST will keep them safe. The demand for our products will grow as never before, thanks to ZENDUST. Crack from us in the evening, ZENDUST in the morning, just like the contraceptive pill for girls, fun and no danger!

"This is a most unexpected but welcome outcome for all our families. We are the two most important families in the cocaine supply business and we must plan how to use this knowledge we have gained from the Douglas girl. This, Senor Gomez, is what my father and I would like to discuss with you today. It is very important to keep the girl here safely. She respects my man Diego and we propose that he should be allowed to accompany her at all times. Therefore, we would wish that you keep them both safe, well and content.

"We also regret the death of your son, Rico. We know that you suspect that my man Diego was responsible. Our information is that Rico was stabbed by a drug dealer who was attacking the girl. Rico intervened but was killed. Diego saw what happened. His priority was to take the girl from the scene as quickly as possible, and that is what he did. We are aware of the identity of the man who killed your son. We can inform you of that name so that you can take your revenge at your leisure."

With that, Carlo took a sip of the chilled water on the table and allowed Fernando Gomez some time to consider the huge implications in what he had just said and, not least, the information about his son's killing. "Your information about the girl and the new opportunity for our main business is very interesting. I will deal with the matter of the killing of my son Rico myself. I do not need your help," replied Gomez.

Carlo thought hard and fast. *Does that mean he knows that Diego killed his boy or does he believe the story I have just told him?* Fernando Gomez remained inscrutable to Carlo's gaze. At length Gomez

133

pronounced his views and as so often before, they were very profound and full of insight into the illegal drug business and their customers.

"We will keep the girl and your man Diego safe and unharmed. I know the girl is valuable and it is better that she has someone here that she can trust.

"As for enabling the world to recognise that ZENDUST means that they can get themselves high on our main cocaine products without danger, then that will require careful handling," he smiled briefly, "we have never advertised for customers for our illegal drugs yet the demand grows all the time. Perhaps the same will happen with ZENDUST. I suggest that we should let things take their own course. Users such as the girl will quickly follow her example and realise the new situation created by ZENDUST. I think that some of our dealers will contact the ZENDUST successes that our friend Dr Douglas is always telling us about and remind them of the highs that they experienced and how they can do it again but without problems. The word will soon spread."

Juan Carioli rose to his feet and responded "You are a wise man, Fernando. We will do as you suggest."

With that, Juan and Carlo thanked Gomez for his wise counsel and returned to their waiting car. They sat in silence for a while and then Juan Carioli spoke. "Gomez is right, the word will spread quickly enough. We need do nothing except wait. The illegal drugs business will be better than ever before."

Father and son were agreed on that.

Fernando Gomez, the wise man, was happy to wait for the right moment to take his revenge on the killer of his son Rico. He knew very well that it was Carlo's man Diego, who was now in the hands of the Gomez family.

Chapter 14
Joey

Joey Jones had been clean of addictive drugs ever since he had completed the ZENDUST programme as one of Dr Douglas' trial batch. He had become something of a star in his own right as a result of his heart-rending account of his resurrection because of ZENDUST during the original press conference in New York. He had often accompanied Douglas to other press conferences around the world where he repeated his story. A book company was now after him and Joey had agreed to sell his story. The advance was half a million dollars. The publishers were confident that sales would be in the millions worldwide and they could see a profit on the way.

Joey was in a different world to the backstreets in which he had grown up. Today they were back in the USA and he was scheduled to appear on another talk show on radio. He did this independently of Douglas now. Listeners and viewers didn't want to hear the technicalities from Douglas, they wanted the true-life story of Joey Jones. Joey knew this, and he was in the money. A completely new experience for a backstreet kid, especially as it was all legal and not the proceeds of a mugging or theft.

Douglas had called Joey to see him recently. "Joey, I have known you now for quite some time and you have done well to get out of the gutter and the awful life of a junkie to where you are now. I know that you are becoming a great star in TV and the media and good luck to you. You will be very rich soon, especially when your book comes out.

"Do me a favour, and yourself a favour too, Joey. Remember how you got here. Don't let all this TV attention and the money go to your head. Many who are now on the ZENDUST programme are rich kids who have too much money and are out looking for fun and kicks, the kind of kicks that only hard drugs can give. You have the money now so the kicks are easier for you to get again. Luckily, you have escaped the habit; I hope and pray that you don't get back on that slow, inexorable treadmill to death from which I rescued you."

Joey was very grateful to Douglas for all he had done. "Do you think I am a fool?" he replied. "I will never be a crackhead again." But as he said these words to Douglas, he knew that he missed like crazy the kicks that coke and crack had given him. The addiction that drove him to desperation had gone, but he remembered the beautiful hazy dream-like world that crack had enabled him to enter, and he missed those sensations. The crack cocaine had been an escape from the dreadful reality of the world he had then occupied. Now it was different. If he did coke now, it would just be a bit of fun.

"Good," said Douglas, "you are my star man and an example to millions. Stay clean and thank God for your good fortune," and with that he put an arm around Joey embracing him like the son he had never had for a moment and left Joey to prepare for the upcoming media performance.

The phone rang. "Mr Jones, the car is waiting."

Joey was used to the star treatment by now and he went down to the lobby where the limo was waiting. The radio interview went just like all the others that Joey had done since New York.

"Mr Jones — or may I call you Joey — we are delighted to have you on our show tonight. You are an example to countless other young folk who are addicted to hard drugs. You and the ZENDUST programme with Dr Douglas have shown others the way to beat addiction, and, as you have said, the way to get your life back on track again. Tell our listeners about how you did it."

Joey recited the same story he had told many times before. He was getting bored with all these repeats but the money he earned for telling the same story to many different programmes was good. The same questions continued, with the same answers from Joey.

Finally, the presenter drew the programme to a halt, saying to Joey, "You are a shining example of what can be achieved by our nation's wonderful youth who now have a chance of beating addiction with ZENDUST. Tell us and our listeners, after your experience with crack cocaine and the battle with addiction that you have won, will you ever do hard drugs again?"

"No sir," replied Joey.

"Thank you, Joey Jones, hero of the war against drugs, and goodnight to all our listeners as we end on such an encouraging note of the victory of good over evil…" The lights faded as the end music began and the credits rolled.

Joey took off the mike and wiped his brow. He was hot and tired in the studio and fed up with repeating his story. As he had said originally in the New York ZENDUST launch conference he was just a poor kid from the backwoods like millions of others. He didn't want all this media crap; he just wanted the cash and to get out of the studio as fast as possible.

"Mr Jones," said the messenger, "your cheque is waiting downstairs, and the limo is outside waiting to take you back to your hotel."

"Can I have cash?" asked Joey.

"Yes sir if that is how you want your fee. It will be ready momentarily."

Minutes later, Joey pocketed the envelope and went out to the waiting limo. He was a kid from the backwoods, cash was what he wanted, not some bank cheque. Greenbacks felt better than bank slips.

He slipped into the back seat of the limo; the driver was a new guy he had never seen before. He was a plant arranged by Carlo Carioli.

"Where to, Joey?" he asked.

"Just drive around for a bit. I need a break from all that media stuff. All these guys telling me how great I am, what a wonderful example, and all that shit."

As he drove, Joey was thinking, *What I really want is a lift like I used to get from crack. The hell with ZENDUST.*

"Hey man, you look all washed up," remarked the driver.

"Yeah, well I am sick of all this TV hype."

"You look like you could do with a lift. You know what? I've been driving the girl Annie, Douglas' daughter. Man, has she got the answer."

"Yeah, what's that?" replied Joey.

"She's been just like you were, hooked! Now she gets to have a fix whenever she wants, then she has the ZENDUST pill, and bingo, all the kicks and none of the licks. She never gets the shakes nor nothing, the pill has cured her of the addiction, but she sure gets all the fun."

Joey thought it all out for himself, "Is that right? She's doing the stuff with no problems?"

"Sure is. I've seen her in the back of the car."

Carlo's man was reeling out the line, and Joey was taking the bait. He had picked the right moment, just as Carlo had instructed.

Joey was quiet for a while, thinking. *That Douglas girl Annie is right, I could do the same, do the stuff too. I'm off the addiction, but I sure liked the highs and now*

140

with ZENDUST I won't get the lows. Why not? I really need a lift.

"You got anything?" Joey asked, his mind made up. "I got whatever you want, man," and he passed back the little white package of heaven that Joey wanted, needed and couldn't refuse. Seeing Joey in the mirror, the driver smiled. Carlo would be pleased when he heard about Joey. He knew now that Joey was back in the habit... the everlasting habit... the killing habit!

The limo delivered Joey back to the apartment he had been renting since he had come into the money. He had lost contact with his family years ago when he became a crackhead. Now he shared the place with a couple of guys off the street.

"Hey Joey, you look bright, you been back on the stuff?" joked one of his mates.

"Hey, you guys, listen to this, I know how you can do the stuff, get your highs but not the lows. The driver told me how Douglas' daughter does it, easy man!

"All you gotta do is get on the ZENDUST programme, get off the addiction, then get your fix of crack or whatever you want and take the ZENDUST the next morning. That gets rid of the addiction but leaves you easy for the highs that you get with the stuff. It's like the morning-after pill for girls who get shagged, take one the next morning and problem solved. What a breeze!"

"That true, man?" they asked.

"Sure is. Why do you think I got like this! It's easy, man," replied Joey.

The word had been planted in fertile ground by Carlo's man.

The news spread fast. The internet chat lines were soon humming, worldwide. Millions of young folk, turned on their computers every day and communicated to every corner and niche on the planet. These were the same young folk who were out at raves every weekend, popping pills and looking for kicks. Most were also sensible to the dangers of getting hooked on anything too strong, but the possibility of ZENDUST as a morning-after pill and hence 'all the kicks with none of the risks' was great news. You couldn't have picked a more receptive audience or a better and more effective way of transmitting the news.

The best joke of all was when they read on the internet that it had been Annie Douglas who had dreamed up the notion of using ZENDUST as a morning-after pill, all the highs and none of the lows were promised. The way was clear to have a go at almost any fix that was going.

"Let's get high!" was the reaction on the chat lines, and as quickly as possible.

Within days, there was a new website called www.havefunwithZENDUST.com getting thousands of hits every hour worldwide.

Solomons and his colleagues at DARC saw the website, realised the implications that demand for

ZENDUST would explode and couldn't believe their luck. The stock price of DARC reached astronomical heights; they were the darlings of Wall Street. They didn't stop for a moment to think of the ethics of a drug which had created a new market for coke and crack.

There was just one thought that crossed their corporate minds and they looked back to the call they had taken from their ethical investor, Carlo Carioli at JC Investments. How had he known a few weeks ago that there was going to be an explosion in demand for ZENDUST when he had urged them to crank up production?

"Anyhow, who cares how this guy Carioli knew," said Solomons, "there certainly had been no call from JC Investments about the ethics of ZENDUST as a morning-after pill."

Luke Simons, CEO at SGB, was in a dilemma. His company, the biggest pharmaceutical company in the world looked like it was missing out on the biggest bonanza drug since Viagra. But he was uneasy. Did he take his company into manufacturing a drug like ZENDUST when the outcome would be a corresponding explosion in the demand for illegal drugs like crack and cocaine which every teenager in the world now thought of as fair game since the risk of addiction had been removed? Would that be ethical? What if he did take SGB into the market with a clone of ZENDUST and then there was a problem. Nobody on his Board of Directors or on Wall Street would thank him then, even if now they were telling him to get the SGB version of ZENDUST out into the market pronto.

John Douglas heard about it and was totally shocked. He couldn't believe what he saw on the website, especially when he read that it had been his own daughter, Annie, who had come up with the morning-after idea. His dreams of doing good by bringing relief to junkies worldwide had been hijacked by his own daughter!

He was suddenly consumed with anger at what his daughter Annie had done. *How* could *she, the stupid fool! How could she get involved with drugs after all I told her and all the work I have done for years. How could she do this to me?* He had never been so angry in all his life; Annie was going to ruin everything. He couldn't speak, he was so overwhelmed.

And another thing, how did she get the idea that ZENDUST was a morning-after pill? I have never said such a thing. The drug has never been tested like that and I certainly don't want to be known as the man who unleashed a new wave of hard-drug users when I have just been so successful in getting rid of so many addicts.

The more he thought about Annie, the angrier he became. ZENDUST was to do good things in the world and now it has been hijacked.

He thought of calling Val, his wife, to talk about it but he hadn't called her for weeks, he had been so busy enjoying the success of ZENDUST. He felt guilty about the time he was spending with the nubile girls operating as his PAs wherever he went and consequently forgetting to call Val. Now Annie had shattered all that good feeling.

Anne has been a load of trouble since the day she was born, he mused. , *"Now she has gone too far, the stupid senseless girl. A morning-after pill, what a load of trouble that will be, especially as it might not work and by the time everyone realises that it will be too late.*

My God," he thought, *"as well as the miracle, I have created a monster."*

It was a nightmare, visited on him by his own daughter.

Chapter 15
Annie

Soon after Annie had come back from her dreamworld, following the fix that she had been given on the plane with Diego, she was taken in to see Fernando Gomez. Annie had no idea where she was, or what had happened... and where was her friend Diego? At least she was getting herself back together after the fix. *Boy that had been quite something,* she thought.

The weather was very hot she noted and looking outside she saw a number of tough-looking men with what looked like heavy-duty guns. This wasn't where she thought she was going with Diego.

A man came into the room where she had been sleeping and said, "Mr Gomez would like to see you now," and he waited for her to come with the door open.

"Who's Mr Gomez," asked Annie, but the man was silent and just guided her into a very large lounge overlooking a beautiful garden, full of flowers in bloom and tinkling fountains fronting a backdrop of spectacular mountains.

An olive-skinned, grey haired and elegantly but casually dressed man was waiting by the window.

"Annie Douglas, you are most welcome to my home. My name is Fernando Gomez and I am a business partner of your father's, in his wonderful ZENDUST project. We knew you had been in some difficulty in England with dealers of cocaine and crack, and we arranged to rescue you from your troubles. No father would like to see his daughter as a hooker selling herself for illegal drugs. We have any drug here that you might need as well as the ZENDUST which will ease the burden of addiction. You know, of course, that if you take ZENDUST after a fix then the addictive urge is eliminated, so the danger of addiction has disappeared. Excuse me if I am a little blunt in what I say but we know that you couldn't obtain the ZENDUST you needed because you were working as a prostitute to satisfy your addiction. As well, you felt unable to ask your father, and we understand your dilemma. We can help you. In this way, you will be able to return to your family and friends as if you had never got involved with backstreet dealers and vicious men willing to turn you onto the streets as a prostitute. Your mother and father know you have gone away for a while and that you will contact them when you wish, so they are happy in that knowledge. They do not know about your recent life and it is better that it should remain so.

"As it is, you can stay here. Your friend Diego is also here to keep your company."

Annie sat down on the sofa; a thousand questions flooded into her head. 'Was this man for real or am I still high?' was the first on the list.

"Can I have some coffee?" she asked.

"Whilst you are my guest in my house, you can have anything you like," replied Gomez, "and I mean anything!" and he rang a small bell which lay on the mantelpiece over a large fire grate. Annie drank the coffee which had arrived on a silver platter brought in by a white-jacketed servant.

This is some magnificent place, she thought to herself. *And this guy is very rich.*

"Please tell me where I am. I can't understand what has happened. The whole set-up seems very strange to me. I start out on the street looking for a man to give me money for sex so I can buy some crack and then something happens. A guy gets shoved into a car, someone else picks me up and takes me to an apartment and talks to me for a while and then gives me another fix. When I wake up, I am here, so where is here?"

"You have come to my ranch in a remote part of Spain." Gomez thought it wiser not to tell Annie she was really in Colombia in South America. If she looked at the TV, she would see the programmes in Spanish so she wouldn't guess, and looking outside, it could easily be Spain.

"You're kidding!" Annie was astounded. "I don't believe you! I don't remember getting on a plane. How did you get me through London Airport?"

"Turn on the TV, if you like. You will see news in Spanish, and you came in my private plane. You were high on drugs at the time."

Annie turned on the TV. He was right, the programmes were in Spanish and the hot sun outside certainly was not English.

"Why am I here? Tell me again?" she asked.

"As I said, I am a business partner in the ZENDUST project. Your father knows very well that if news gets out that his own daughter is an addict and a prostitute then his credibility as a saviour of other addicts from illegal drugs would be ruined and, along with that, the business in which we have invested would be destroyed. He has asked me to help you get over the addiction by giving you ZENDUST and to ensure that while you are getting better you have access to the illegal drugs you may want without going onto the streets as a common prostitute."

Fernando Gomez had learned to lie convincingly many years ago as a kid when he had frequently been picked up by the police but had never given them any useful information in spite of being beaten up in the cells on several occasions.

Annie thought about the things this man was telling her. *It makes sense,* she thought, *"but I need some time to know what to ask next.*

"Can I go and have a bath or a shower or something? I need some time to sort my mind out."

"Certainly, I have a maid who will help you," said Gomez and he smiled kindly at Annie. "You will be safe here and free of problems soon."

He touched the ball again, and a maid appeared promptly. He spoke rapidly to her in what sounded to Annie very much like Spanish.

"Go with her," said Gomez to Annie, "and I will see you later."

Annie still couldn't quite get her mind round what had happened to her, but she followed the maid out and along some panelled corridors into a large and luxurious bathroom. This was the second luxurious bathroom she had been to within the space of a day or two. *No wonder I am totally confused,* she thought to herself. She stripped off her clothes and stepped into the shower, feeling the hot spray stinging her body and enabling her to clear her mind of the after-effects of her last fix. She asked the maid to leave her alone, but she wouldn't go. She just sat in the corner of the bathroom, looking like some sort of minder or guard thought Anne as the water washed over her. The shower had done the job; her mind was clearer now and she felt good in her body. The last vestiges of her encounters with punters who had paid to fuck her had been washed away and she thanked God that she was not out on the streets again being pawed at by punters and harassed by dealers.

She put on a white bathrobe that the maid held out ready and followed her back to the room where she had woken up earlier. The maid offered her a drink which she drank down without stopping. It was one of the after-effects of a fix and Annie always woke up thirsty. She immediately felt drowsy. She lay back on the bed and she was asleep in minutes. The maid noted that all had gone as she had been instructed, and went out of the room, locking it behind her. Gomez was pleased when the maid reported that Annie had been no trouble and that all had gone to plan. The sleeping draught would keep Annie quiet for several hours.

Fernando Gomez was not the kind of person to spend long hours looking at a computer and the internet, so he had no knowledge that Annie was becoming as famous as her father, but for a very different reason.

He had not looked at www.havefunwithZENDUST.com, but thousands had around the world. The internet was a magic device which reached to the far corners of every country on the globe instantly. Carlo Carioli had seen it and was astounded!! Although he hated the Gomez family with all his being, he could now see the wisdom of the words that Gomez had spoken when they had last met in that tense discussion only a few days ago.

Gomez had been right; the word had spread without anybody doing anything. Annie had done it all for them, telling Carlo what had happened to her and getting the word to Joey just at the right moment. He would have to speak to Gomez again; the matter of his son's killing had not been resolved. Diego was still the number-one suspect in Gomez's mind.

Chapter 16
The Judgement of Solomons

Douglas decided he had to call Solomons at DARC and put a stop to all this nonsense being promulgated by www.havefunwithZENDUST.com. It was outrageous, the antithesis of all that he had worked for in ZENDUST. He had set out to do some good in the world and he didn't want it all to collapse inwards, like the aftermath of some volcano that suddenly runs out of its fiery energy and then implodes to a quiescent lake as if it had never existed. Douglas thought that if he could meet up with Solomons then a new press release could be made to dismiss the possibilities of fun without the cost, the message that was being put about by the website.

He called the DARC HQ and was told that Solomons was very busy but would call him back as soon as he was free. That had been two days ago and Douglas had counted the hits on www.havefunwithZENDUST.com, now running into the millions. He called again. Suzanne, Solomons' PA, answered as usual, saying, "Oh, hi John, yes we know about your call and all that stuff on the website. The demand for ZENDUST is going crazy and we are cranking up production as fast as we can. Mr Solomons is free on Friday though and it would be great if you could come over then."

"I'll be there," said Douglas and put the phone back on the hook. He was fuming. Didn't Solomons realise that the last thing he wanted was to crank up production? He should be out there on TV talking about the dangers of ZENDUST as a panacea for hard drugs, not cashing in on the opportunity for new business and yet more profits. That was typical of Solomons and DARC, they were all only interested in the bottom line showing large profits.

Douglas had tried to call his daughter Annie but no one seemed to know where she was. Feeling frustrated now, he phoned Val, and she told him some garbled story about South Americans coming to her house and helping to find Annie although Val hadn't heard from Annie for several days.

Val had been very angry with him too. She had heard all about www.havefunwithZENDUST.com and she had had the press reporters knocking at her door and phoning at all times of the day and night. They all wanted to know what she thought about this new freedom to use drugs and, at the same time, be protected by ZENDUST. She blamed John. The whole thing was becoming a nightmare. ZENDUST had killed her previous life. That pleasant life with Annie, John, her job in the boutique and their nice little home was rapidly becoming a thing of the past, or so it seemed to Val.

John sat in his hotel room. He was back in New York, where it had all started. Sitting in the same hotel, he was feeling lonely, angry and frustrated, especially with Annie. What was Annie doing getting mixed up in the drug culture and then saying ZENDUST is great because everyone can take what they like? Not to mention Val, who seemed to resent the whole idea of his success. *Well fuck them,* he thought. *I can't believe I am so angry and frustrated now when I had been so exhilarated at the ZENDUST Press Launch here in this same hotel!*

He went down to the bar. It was getting late and he ordered a large whisky. There was a good selection of single malts and, being a Scotsman, he knew exactly which one he liked. He sat at the bar and contemplated all that had happened since he was last here. The whisky didn't last long and another appeared as if by magic. He looked around and saw an attractively dressed blonde woman also sitting alone, and he deliberately caught her eye. She smiled and raised her glass to him. He smiled back.

God, he thought, *I could do with some company tonight,* and he gestured to the woman to offer her a refill of her drink. She smiled again, and as she moved to sit next to him, he could smell the heady scent of her perfume and he could see the swell of her breasts over the top of the dress she was wearing under her black leather jacket. "Would you like a drink? he asked, although it sounded so banal.

She smiled again and leaned towards him letting her breast touch his arm. "Tequila cocktail would be great. My name is Lisa, and yours?"

"John," he said as he ordered the cocktail and another whisky for himself. He was beginning to feel somewhat lightheaded, intoxicated by the whisky and by the thought of this woman Lisa, naked and in his bed.

She moved a little closer and put her hand on his thigh, "Are you in New York for long?" she asked. She was well-practised in the art of casual conversation.

"Just a few days," he replied. "It's a great city, full of action all day and all night."

"I've been here for two years and I have loved every minute." She went on casually, sipping her drink, "Are you staying in this hotel?"

"Yes. I've stayed here before. It's really a very good hotel and I have a room on the 12th floor."

The conversation was a complete illusion. Lisa and John both knew the unspoken outcome they both sought. He to fuck her and she to get the cash. He cut short the chat; it was so meaningless. He didn't need the chat, he wanted sex.

"Look, Lisa, I am in room 1254, would you like to join me there?"

"Sure thing, do you have the money?"

"Yes, see you in a moment," and he left her sitting there whilst he went to the elevator. She finished her drink and went over to the bathroom to fix her make-up and adjust her dress.

Moments later, John heard the quiet tap on his door. Checking through the peephole, he saw it was Lisa and he opened the door full of anticipation of what she might offer. As she came in, he saw that she had pulled down the top of her blouse so that he got a good view of her full white breasts spilling out almost to the tops of her rouged nipples. She was looking so sexy! She was smart. She had seen it all before, she knew it was exactly what he wanted. He was hooked by the hooker.

For a moment, a picture of Val flashed through his mind but he shut the door after Lisa, grabbing her, he held her close, squashing those lovely tits against his hardening body, and all thoughts of Val vanished from his consciousness.

The next morning, Lisa had gone and it was back to reality for John Douglas. Lisa called Carlo Carioli from the hotel and told him what had happened.

"Good," he said and cut off the phone with an inward smile. Douglas would be easy meat for the Carioli family when the time came to apply some pressure, as it surely would. He thought about it for a moment and then composed a short email for Solomons to read when he arrived at his office the next morning:

"For the personal attention of Mr D Solomons, Chairman, DARC.

We have information that your Dr John Douglas had a prostitute in his hotel room last night. As ethical investors in DARC and ZENDUST, we should warn you that this behaviour of your star employee is inappropriate.

Mr C Carioli, JC Ethical Investors Inc"

Solomons read it first thing.

How the hell does Carioli know about Douglas? he thought at first, then second, *"What a stupid bastard that Douglas is; a hooker, by God!"*

John's meeting with Solomons was fixed for that afternoon. He wanted to be sure he got his message over about the dangers of www.havefunwithZENDUST.com. He was still so angry about ZENDUST being hijacked by being used as a 'morning-after' pill. Sex with Lisa last night had been just what he needed to take his mind off his frustrations but it had only been a temporary diversion.

Expensive but worth it, he thought. He hadn't thought any more of Val sitting back home in England. He had however thought a lot about Annie. He could hardly stop thinking about her, and what she had done to him and his ZENDUST by inventing the idea of the 'morning-after' pill. Thoughts of Annie nearly drove him to apoplexy. How could she have done this to him? It was all so unfair.

He was at the DARC offices promptly. Suzanne said that Mr Solomons was already in a meeting about production targets for ZENDUST and asked him to wait. Douglas could feel his anger boiling over when he heard that. Production targets for ZENDUST was not the important issue right now, he thought. The issue was what to do about the website and the 'morning-after pill' idea. He sat and fumed for thirty-five minutes before the door of Solomons' office opened and members of the ZENDUST production team filed out, looking harassed and browbeaten as staff members usually did after a session with the boss.

"Hi there, John," breezed Solomons, "Suzanne told me you had been calling, what's the problem? Come right in and sit down."

Douglas followed him into the plush office and stood in front of the large mahogany desk where Solomons held sway.

"The problem is this website www.havefunwithZENDUST.com and the illusion that ZENDUST can be used as a morning-after pill. This is not what ZENDUST is about. I did this to help hardcore addicts to a new way of life not to give an open door for everyone to do coke, crack and God alone knows what else without a care in the world. You must put a stop to it, and right now!" He was almost shouting as all his frustrations of the last few days came to the surface.

"Hey, hey, hold on, John. Calm down and sit down; I can't handle talking to you whilst you are standing and shouting at me." There was an edge to his voice that Douglas failed completely to pick up. "Suzanne, bring in a couple of coffees, please," he said, giving John a few moments to calm down. Douglas sat down, as Suzanne came in with the coffees. She was quick, she knew when her boss wanted instant action.

"What is going on is absolutely outrageous—" he began again, but Solomons cut him short.

"Listen to me, John. I am the chairman of DARC. We funded all your work when you couldn't find anyone else with cash. You have come up with ZENDUST, just as we wanted, and now we are going to get our payback. If people want a morning-after pill and we have what they want in ZENDUST, then they are going to get it. Of course, the crackheads will get what they need too but if there is a big market out there then we will go for it. We are a business, not a fucking hospital!" As he spoke, he regretted his choice of words, but Douglas had to shape up. This was payback time, and Douglas and whoever would have to come to terms with it. DARC would not give up this opportunity of a lifetime.

"Have you got the message, John?" he went on. "This is a business, not a fucking research project for your Nobel Prize. And one last thing, what the hell were you doing with a hooker in your room last night? If she goes to the media, then you are certainly history. There'll be no more love affair with the UN or the media for you. What's more, it will do ZENDUST's reputation and DARC's share price no good at all if you are seen to be an idiot who can't keep his dick in his pants! Your personal share options will take a dive and nobody will care a fig."

Douglas was dumbfounded. Devastated. Humiliated. All at the same time. How could they possibly know about Lisa? It had only been a few hours ago. And the other things. He loved the adulation he was getting from his colleagues, the high life as a media superstar and he frequently calculated the profits he could make from his options. He sat down heavily, not knowing quite how to respond or even what to say at all.

He realised that Solomons was in control. He was the decision-maker. It was out of Douglas' hands, and this was the judgement of Solomons on him, whatever he might have to say. John Douglas may have fucked Lisa last night, but he was impotent today with Solomons.

Chapter 17
Val's Decision

Back in John's little house in England, Val woke that same morning feeling tired and fed up as she seemed to be every day now. She hadn't been sleeping well for weeks now and had been to the doctor to get some stronger sleeping pills. The ones she had bought over the counter hadn't worked. The doctor had warned her not to take more than one each night, "These are very strong and I don't normally prescribe them but I know the difficulties you are going through at the moment. Just be careful," he had said.

It had been like that ever since the phone call from Annie saying she was OK but with no word of where she was or how Val could get in touch. There hadn't been a word from her since, and the South American lad Diego seemed to have disappeared too. She often thought of Diego with a mixture of regret at having made herself so available to him tinged with the slightly uncomfortable feelings of how much she had enjoyed being well and truly fucked by him. After all, she consoled herself, John was never at home these days and when she tried to call him it was always some attractive-sounding personal assistant who took her message and said John would call back, but he hardly ever did. Sometimes, actually quite often now, she wondered if he had been sleeping with these girls. After all, so many men did when they were away on business or so she had read in the Sunday newspapers and her friends were always telling her about their wayward husbands. She also wondered that if he had slept with some of these girls, what they would have been like in bed. What with the family and jobs, it had been difficult for their sex life to be as free as she would have liked, and she wondered if John had felt the same way? Perhaps that's why he never called; he was too busy getting sex without any responsibilities...

She would try again. She picked up the phone by her bedside. She knew he was in New York at the same hotel where he had given the original press conference which had been so successful and started the rollercoaster that he was riding with so much enjoyment.

"Dr Douglas, please. He is a guest there."

"Good afternoon, Madam. I will put you through directly."

A girl's voice answered. "Dr Douglas' suite, who is speaking please?"

Val was immediately angry; what was a girl doing in his suite??

"It's his wife."

"I'm sorry, Dr Douglas is in a meeting right now. I will tell him you called and he will call back later," and the phone went dead.

Val's frustrations boiled over; who the hell was this girl to say that her husband wouldn't speak to her, what a damn cheek!! What was she doing in his room anyway!!

She redialled immediately.

"Dr Douglas' suite, who is speaking please?"

"It's his wife and don't cut me off, put me through to him directly!"

"Hello, who's that?" John sounded so angry and annoyed at having been interrupted in his room. He had just got back from his meeting with Solomons at DARC and he was in no mood for a chat.

"Hello John, it's Val."

"Oh. Hi Val. Look, this isn't the right moment. I'll call you back later."

"John. It never seems the right moment these days. When will you be back home? We really do need to talk. I have reporters and TV cameras parked outside my door harassing me constantly. They won't go away. And I am so worried about Annie."

The mention of Annie was the trigger for Douglas. He exploded with anger and frustration. "Annie is a stupid fucking brat. I don't know or care what she is up to, except I hope we never hear about her again in my whole life. I am very busy here so please stop calling

163

me. I won't be able to get away. I'll call you when I can!" and he slammed down the phone.

Val was devastated and dumbfounded, just as her husband had been a few hours before at the confrontation at DARC. John wouldn't even talk to her.

She collapsed into tears, sobbing violently, lying alone in the bed where they had conceived their daughter, gathering the bedclothes around her, missing the warmth of a man beside her. She wondered if the girl on the phone had actually been in bed with John at that moment, raising her husband to a climactic sexual ecstasy, whilst she was alone, cold and crying.

She realised now that her life was in ruins, John wouldn't come home and he was extremely angry with Annie for a reason that Val couldn't fathom. He didn't seem to care if he never saw Annie again, or, it seemed to Val, herself.

She had no part in his life any more. And Annie never called although she had said she would. John and Annie had filled her life before. Now, it seemed, she had nothing left to live for.

It was enough to make her feel suicidal.

She would have stayed in bed all day except she heard the dog Rags barking. He wanted his morning walk and, to be honest, she thought to herself, Rags was the only living being who was showing her any affection at all these days.

She roused herself unwillingly out her bed and went downstairs. Rags was delighted to see her, as always, and jumped up barking and tail wagging. She pushed him down and got his food from the fridge. The dog ate hungrily, as he always did. As she watched Rags eat, she mused about all the times she had prepared breakfast for John before he had gone out to the university and for Annie before school. All that was finished now. It would never return, she knew. She couldn't stop her tears beginning again.

Rags pushed the food bowl around the kitchen floor in a vain attempt, to lick up any remaining atoms of food that he might have missed. He realised that the bowl was perfectly clean, reluctantly gave up on food, picked up his lead in his mouth and stood in front of Val wagging his tail and waiting for the walk which always followed food.

Wiping the tears from her eyes, Val went back to her lonely bedroom, quickly dressed and went downstairs to open the front door for Rags and herself to confront the world. It was raining, the dark clouds matching her mood.

They walked out across the park, and as she did so, she remembered the meetings with Diego. It had been wonderful for her to have someone to talk to. Nowadays, no one seemed to have time to chat to her. All her friends were busy getting on with their lives, planning their holidays for next year, taking the sons or daughters to parties, doing the family shopping, all the everyday things. Val had no everyday things. Nothing. She only had Rags to care for, or who cared about her, it seemed.

Val called Rags as they neared the gate of the park. They always walked back past the shops along the busy main road and Rags needed to be put on the lead. As always, he pulled violently against the lead, Rags was a dog who disliked any kind of restraint. He practically towed Val along the road and past the newsagents. As they passed, Val caught a glimpse of the headlines splashed over the front page: *Local scientist Dr John Douglas of ZENDUST fame, caught in sex romp with prostitute.*

Val was transfixed. She read it again, as if it wasn't true the first time. But it was there, front page, for all to see. It was a disaster. Everyone she knew would read it. No wonder the press had called to her house this morning but as she had done a hundred times before, she had told them to get lost without asking why they were there yet again.

She dropped the dog's lead without thinking, she was so totally absorbed in the newspaper headlines. It surely couldn't be true, it must be a story, but there it was, for everyone to see. Now all her friends would be reading about how her husband had gone off with a common prostitute, as if Val was an inadequate wife and lover, and talking about her behind her back. She felt awful. She had sometimes thought that John had been involved with the pretty young assistants who always seemed to be with him when she called, but a cheap prostitute! A common hooker! Whatever John may have done before, this was worse and to read about it in the papers without him even warning her… it was too awful to contemplate…

Val was transfixed by what she read. She had visions of all the appalling personal questions that she would have to face when the papers were seen by all her friends, and they read about her husband's sex romps with a cheap hooker. For long moments, her mind was completely dysfunctional, and inadvertently her hands had come loose, letting free the dog's lead.

Rags realised immediately that he was free and shot across the road. Val vaguely heard the squeal of brakes and a dull thud. Rags was knocked flying, back across the road and landed right in front of Val, with his head strangely sideways. Val saw, as if in a dream, that Rags had blood oozing from his ears and head. He seemed to look straight at her. His appealing black-and-yellow eyes focused sadly on her as if he was accusing her of deliberately dropping his lead and letting him run out to be hit by the truck. She watched horrified as the light in Rags' eyes faded, his breath escaping in a deep sigh, and then he was dead, right at Val's feet.

The only living thing that cared for her was dead, at her feet. And she had caused it. She had killed her only living friend. It was a dreadful, cathartic and decisive moment, as if the headlines in the papers weren't enough. People crowded round, asking her if she was all right. Val couldn't think of anything except that Rags was dead and it was her own fault. If only she hadn't seen that newspaper headline… if only Annie had been there... if only John had never invented ZENDUST... if... if... if

She saw them put Rags in a black bag, just as if he was just another pile of useless rubbish. Val couldn't stand to be there any longer, and she rushed away before anyone could talk to her or before the police came. She raced home; her mind was made up. Her decision was absolute. Rags had gone, along with her whole life as she had known it. Annie, John, marriage, her former life, everything she had known and worked for and cared for... now Rags as well... was finished. She had nothing left for which to live.

Val had now no hesitation. She opened her front door, leaving it swinging on the latch, and went immediately upstairs. She sat on the double bed, took out the sleeping pills that the doctor had prescribed, and began to swallow them, one after the other, deliberately and determinedly. She also took a large drink of the brandy that John had brought home from his last trip. As she ate the pills, she took her notepad, and began writing... her last letter to John... her husband for all those years ... and to her lovely Annie... her suicide note... to say, *'It's over... I can't take it any more... there is nothing left for me... ZENDUST gave you the life you wanted, John... but ruined mine... it seems so strange that I should be taking pills to finish it all... so be it... love to Annie... she hasn't called... and I... I love you both... more than you ever knew... goodbye... XX.'*

She felt strange... and dizzy... and sleepy... The pen slipped from her hand... just as Rags' lead had earlier... she remembered that terrible moment... she was slipping back onto the bed... at last a time of peace came...

The police called two hours later to ask her about the accident involving Rags. They found the front door unlocked... and Val Douglas dead upstairs, in the bed she had shared with John for all those years. They found John's mobile number in Val's handbag.

"May I speak to Mr John Douglas?"

"Can I take a message; he is busy right now?" said the young-sounding woman on the other end.

"No. It is very important. A personal matter. I am a police officer."

"Just a moment, please."

"Hello, Douglas here," John answered abruptly, wondering what trouble Annie or Val had got into now. That was usually what had happened when the police had called him before.

"Mr Douglas, I have some bad news. We would normally have visited you in person in such cases. I have to tell you that your wife, Mrs Val Douglas, was found dead this afternoon at your house. It appears that she committed suicide. There is a note. You are requested to return to England without delay as suicides are initially police matters."

John was dumbfounded. For the second time that day. Speechless.

"Mr Douglas, are you there?"

He tried to gather himself together as he absorbed the news. "Yes, can you give me a few minutes… I will call you back. Give my secretary the number. Thank you." The police officer thought that Douglas' response was somewhat strange. Usually when he had given news like this, the recipient had burst into tears or wanted to ask endless questions: how? Why? Where? When?

John sat down heavily. He had great trouble determining what his real feelings were at the news. He poured a large whisky and pondered the news, in a rather dispassionate sort of manner, quite unlike what would be normal for a man who had just been informed that his wife had killed herself.

In reality, he thought, *I haven't seen Val for weeks, and our sex life is over. I am in a different world now. Val had never liked the world I live in now. Annie seems to have gone on to make trouble for everyone. I hope she stays lost. I am sorry for Val, but it was her decision, not mine. So be it.*

And so, he made his decision. He asked his pretty secretary to call the police back.

"Tell them, that it is quite impossible for me to return to England at present as I have extremely important business to attend to in relation to millions of drug addicts trying to escape death or suicide. They can deal with my lawyer if there are any questions."

With that terse message, Val joined Annie in being eliminated from the mind of Dr John Douglas.

Chapter 18
Ups and Downs

Carlo Carioli read about the suicide of Val Douglas and considered it very carefully, as he always did when things happened that were connected with the business interests of himself and his father through JC Investments.

He had never met the woman and if she chose to kill herself, then so be it. What really mattered was whether John Douglas was becoming a problem.

This was the second time he had read about Douglas in the media, the other one being when his girl Lisa had talked to the press about her '*Night of sex with the ZENDUST star*'.

She would, he knew, never do that again. He had told her never to talk to the press but she had, and now she had paid the penalty for disobeying him. Lisa was dead and forgotten.

The ZENDUST business was like a roller coaster, especially now that the 'morning-after' effect had taken hold worldwide. The Carioli and Gomez families were busily feeding the illegal drugs like crack cocaine into the hands of all those who would now snort, sniff, smoke and inject quite happily, confident that all would be OK when they took ZENDUST the next day.

Carioli and the five families controlling the hard-drug supply business and, as investors in DARC and ZENDUST, had never been so rich. The amounts of hard cash coming in to the hands and the value of their shares in DARC was incredible. In fact, Carlo, in his Harvard Business School fashion, calculated that the income into the five families was greater than that of many countries.

Carlo was very sensitive to the prospect that John Douglas would generate more unwelcome news for the international media to probe and publish. None of the families wanted anybody investigating their business although it was becoming very difficult to launder all the cash coming in from cocaine and crack. He consulted his father, but Juan was content to live in his luxury villa and leave matters of irritating personnel such as Lisa and Douglas up to Carlo.

Carlo decided to call Fernando Gomez.

"Senor Gomez, you may have heard that the scientist Dr Douglas has caused some unwelcome headlines in the media. My father and I think that this risk of media attention should not be allowed to continue. We would also like to thank you for your wise advice about publicising the use of ZENDUST as a 'morning-after' pill. Your judgement was perfectly correct. News like that travels fast amongst the users of our products, and the result is that now we are supplying

173

more cocaine than ever before and at the same time earning substantial returns from our investments in ZENDUST and DARC Inc. You will have seen the statements and financial information from your bankers."

"Thank you, Carlo" came the typically solemn response from Fernando Gomez.

Carlo continued. "We now consider that Dr Douglas has done everything we require for ZENDUST at present. The drug works and is in full scale production. We do not need him to publicise the beneficial effects any more. All our users know that very well. We intend to instruct DARC to move Douglas to a role where he will not be permitted press contact. He will not then be a problem. Is this in accordance with your wishes?"

Gomez was silent for a few minutes, and then answered, "I agree, you may do as you propose with the man Douglas. I have as well two other matters which we need to resolve between our families. I have the girl Annie. She is of no value to me. Please accept her into your care.

"Secondly, my son Rico's death has not been resolved. I have your man Diego, whom I believe was responsible. We do not want any difficulties about such matters to come between our families, as in the vendettas of the old days. It is better that you, Carlo Carioli as the new *patrone* of the family, confirm that Diego was responsible, and then he will be dealt with by my family."

Carlo was in his turn silent for a few minutes, giving himself time to consider what should be done. Diego and himself went back a long way. They had been friends since childhood. Diego's father had been killed by a rival gang to the Carioli's and he had never known his mother. Carlo's father had ensured retribution for the killing. No servant of the family could be killed with impunity. He had given Diego a home, and Carlo and Diego had been in many scrapes as the Carioli business prospered in the illegal drugs trade to the USA. There was however no alternative; Rico's death required retribution and Diego had to be sacrificed. Carlo made the inevitable decision.

"Senor Gomez. We believe also that Diego killed Rico. It is true that I sent Diego to England but I gave him no instructions to kill your esteemed son Rico. It was Diego's personal responsibility, not that of the Carioli family. Vengeance for your son Rico is yours to take from Diego. It is good that no one knows where Diego is being held and we do not wish to hear his name mentioned ever again. He is in your hands.

"Business is very good for the families and peace exists. We wish for no violent vendettas. It should continue that way."

"Thank you for your honesty, Carlo Carioli," and the line went dead.

Carlo knew that Diego was now a dead man. Unfortunately, business came first.

He turned away to make a call to Solomons at DARC.

Fernando Gomez called his bodyguard and asked him to bring Diego to him.

Diego had known from the day that he had fallen into the hands of the Gomez family that he was a dead man walking. When the guard unchained him from the room in which he had been kept and told him that Senor Gomez wished to talk to him, he knew the moment had come and that his time was up. He was pushed roughly up from his basement prison and into the presence of Fernando Gomez. His guard standing close by, a heavy revolver in his hand.

The bleak eyes of Gomez stared at him coldly as he was manhandled into a chair and chained securely to the base. He did not speak for several minutes as he studied the face of the man who had killed his son, Rico. Diego was unused to the feeling of fear, but he felt the chill presence of death now, as never before.

"Diego, I do not know your family name. My son Rico is dead and we have confirmed that you are the killer. Justice must be done, your life for that of my son, although you are not worthy to be considered in the same light. I have not the inclination to make you suffer a long and cruel death, it is enough for me that you should be snuffed out like an annoying fly that I might swat. You are nothing. I have no time to waste on you," and he signalled to his guard.

The guard took out his heavy pistol, stood in front of Diego, so that he could see the cold blue steel of the barrel focused between his eyes, waited a moment, and then pulled the trigger. The blast reverberated through the room, Diego's head disintegrated and his brains splashed against the back of the chair, white, bloody and bony. Fernando Gomez looked on for a moment, crossed himself in the Catholic tradition, and left the guard to clear up the mess and dispose of the remains such that nothing would ever be seen or heard of again concerning Diego.

Gomez then went directly to see Annie. "You are going to stay with a family with whom I am on good terms," he said, and left the room.

Fernando Gomez felt that he had satisfied some, but certainly not all, of his needs to avenge his son. He was determined to see that Carlo Carioli would ultimately suffer for his part in what happened to Rico, however long it might take. *Carlo Carioli will never escape the patient and deadly vengeance of the Gomez family* was the thought that was in his head every moment of every day.

The ZENDUST business was going well; his production of cocaine and derivatives was going well, what need did he have to involve himself with such as Annie Douglas or the likes of Diego? Annie was becoming a liability for Gomez now he had dealt with Diego and a potential embarrassment. Maybe it was better that she should go to the Cariolis and they could decide what to do with her.

At the same moment, Solomons was receiving the call from Carlo.

"Good morning, Mr Carioli. I trust you are happy with the results of your investment into our company and our ZENDUST product?" he began, expecting just another routine call from a shareholder in DARC. They were always looking for reassurance about progress.

"Mr Solomons? In answer to your question, yes, we are happy about the financial performance, but there is a very disturbing matter which I and my colleagues wish to have resolved. We are unhappy with what we are reading in the media about Dr Douglas. Prostitutes and suicides are not good for our reputation as ethical investors in companies. We require that he be moved to a less visible position where he is not of interest to the media. He has done his work, ZENDUST is accepted worldwide and he is not now so important. Please recognise, Mr Solomons, that JC Investments is a major shareholder in DARC as a result of our interest in ZENDUST, and we are in a position to ensure that your company implements our recommendations. Please let me know what actions you take to comply with our views."

Solomons was about to reply when he realised that the call had been terminated. He knew very well that as a result of the phenomenal success of ZENDUST, and the terms of the investment by JC, that their equity position was building up to a level whereby they could readily acquire the whole of DARC if they so wished. He had no wish to let that happen, or to see more bad publicity caused by that stupid shit Douglas. That unfortunate publicity has had the effect of dragging down the share price and, with it, Solomons' own net worth.

He called his PA, Suzanne, "Get Douglas here right away," he instructed.

John was at the hotel preparing for a rescheduled meeting at the UN to discuss the UNZAP programme, although he had an uneasy feeling that the UN meeting had another and unpleasant agenda, namely his private life, the suicide of his wife, his daughter Annie, that business of ZENDUST as a morning-after pill, and the incident with the prostitute, Lisa. He was acutely aware of a number of black clouds on his personal horizon.

The call from Suzanne only added to his misgivings, but he said he would be there right away. Suzanne said Mr Solomons would see him immediately he arrived at the DARC office, there was to be no delay.

"Hi there Mr Solomons," he began breezily.

"Sit down John, we have things to talk about, and I have no time to waste on crap. You must know that your lifestyle and family problems are becoming serious problems to our business. We cannot let that continue. We know that you have done a great job in bringing ZENDUST into existence. It's different now, ZENDUST has transmuted into a business concern, not a research project or a social charity. You have done the job we funded, and you are getting your rewards through the DARC equity incentive scheme. We cannot have our business affected by your private life. You have become too close to the media. As of today, you have been reassigned from your present job to a role looking after the clinic for addicts that we have in New Mexico. No media are allowed into that facility, so there should be no more problems in relation to press stories concerning you which is bad for our business. Joe Fredericks will take over as head of ZENDUST and the UNZAP programme. Suzanne will give you the details. That's all," and dismissing John Douglas from his mind, he turned away to the pile of papers on his desk.

John could scarcely move with astonishment.

"John, are you deaf? And still here? Get out of my office now! Suzanne will give you the details of your new assignment as you leave!"

John Douglas' life was imploding fast. From the family man, media star and worldwide saviour for drug addicts of a short while ago, he now had no wife, a daughter who had expanded the future for his ZENDUST in a wholly unacceptable way, no media contracts to exploit and his responsibilities reduced to a nondescript role in the backwoods of New Mexico.

His rise had been stratospheric, but his downfall was becoming even more rapid and precipitous. He had no idea where Annie was and it was the first time for ages that he felt the need to talk to his daughter.

In Medellin, Annie now found herself removed from the room where she had lived rather contentedly for the past few weeks. She no longer had a desperate need to get stoned every night. In fact, with a supply of ZENDUST every morning and the access she had enjoyed to every variation of cocaine each evening courtesy of the Gomez family, she had evolved into the first person in the world to be able to regularly enjoy hardcore drugs without fear and as easily as anyone else might go out and buy a loaf of bread. She cared for herself now in a way she hadn't before, and as she looked into the mirror, she was glad her dowdy student style had passed away and the clothes she had found in the wardrobe had been more stylish.

Annie's idea of ZENDUST as a morning-after pill had opened the door to a risk-free drug culture. Her dad had inadvertently created the opportunity, Annie was the first to recognise it.

The hit you get from cocaine of cocaine could, and would, now be enjoyed by millions without the downside of addiction. The number of hits to www.havefunwithZENDUST.com testified to the truth of her perception. Carlo was well aware of the impact of her website and the worldwide power of social media.

When Annie arrived, he was even more pleased when he saw that, far from being a thin, emaciated ex-crack addict, she was alert, bright and good-looking. This was just the company he needed after the difficult decision concerning Diego.

"My name is Carlo and you are welcome to my home. I think we have every comfort here that you may want," and he took Annie's hand and led her into his house.

"Thank you, kind sir," replied Annie, remembering the manners that had been instilled into her by her mother years ago, and she gave him a warm smile which illuminated the whole of her face, from her chin to her blue eyes. He looked at her as he followed her into the house, thinking, *So this is the girl who is about to make crack and all our other cocaine derivatives accessible to all. She looks great, and what a story she has to tell. Everyone will want to talk to her; the media, TV and everyone will just love her.*

Carlo Carioli had an inspiration at that moment of looking at Annie. He recognised the opportunity as quickly as you would expect from a Harvard graduate.

In his mind's eye, he could see that Annie was about to supplant her father as a media star. The media preferred a good-looking girl with a story of sex, drugs, troubles and happy outcomes, not some middle-aged professor droning on as if he was giving a university lecture, however well-intentioned he might be, and he, Carlo Carioli, was going to make it happen. It was just the sort of stimulus he needed, a new business adventure.

Carlo Carioli and Annie Douglas, what a team they would be! He was delighted to welcome Annie to his home.

For him, the bad feelings of allowing his friend Diego to be killed were suddenly forgotten and magically turned into the fascinating prospect of Annie Douglas.

Chapter 19
Annie's Press Conference

So many people had accessed www.havefunwithZENDUST.com that Annie Douglas was now the person that every newspaper, TV channel and radio station in the world wanted to interview.

The media scrum easily surpassed the attendance at the John Douglas' ZENDUST launch a few short months ago. That one was seen to be mainly of interest to a few crackheads and governments keen to reduce their expenditure on treating addicts and dealing with all the petty crime that went with drug addicts trying to feed their habits. That time lots of people were interested but the number who were directly affected was minuscule.

This time it was completely different. Now absolutely everyone was interested. You could tell from the millions who accessed the website knowing that the awful addictive consequences of sampling hard drugs had, at a stroke, been removed. This time everyone who was curious about the fantastical hallucinogenic worlds of tranquillity, ecstasy or separation from the world experienced by the addicts of old could do the same. A new wonderful and safe freedom! Who could fail to be interested!

Annie had learnt of her mother's suicide from her new friend Carlo Carioli. At first, she had broken down and cried. Daughters are always close to their mothers in spirit even though they often battled against each other, the daughter looking for freedom and an independent life, the mother fearful of what might happen if the daughter was too wayward. Mother and daughter loved each the more for the experiences of conflict and harmony that they had shared.

John had tried to call her but she had refused to take the call. When that happened several times, he had the very uneasy feeling that it was rather like the times when his wife Val had tried to speak to him on the phone and he had been too busy.

The news of Val's suicide had hardened Annie's heart to a concrete-like consistency towards her father, since, as far as she could see, he had completely neglected her mother from the time he had become famous with ZENDUST. Not only that but the headlines of him having sex with a prostitute would have been so awful for her mother that Annie was hardly surprised at Val's decision.

Annie could remember the short time she had been forced out on the streets as a hooker looking for a punter in order to buy a fix. The men she had encountered were sleazy inadequates, pawing at her and wanting her to do all sorts of revolting things to them, so the thought of her father being like them had only strengthened her attitude towards him.

So she had decided to hold her press conference in the very same room that her father had occupied so recently.

How about that then, Dad? How do you like it? It's my turn now! she thought. It had been Carlo Carioli who had thought up the whole idea of a press conference. Annie couldn't quite make out where Carioli had come from or how he had suddenly infiltrated into her life, but he certainly knew how to make things happen.

At first, she had just taken to her new surroundings quite naturally and without any real questions; after all, she had been with that strange but rather kindly old man Fernando Gomez. For a while she had enjoyed the fixes she fancied and the ZENDUST pills for the morning after. It had been rather an idyllic life, no money required and a maid who seemed to be able to sort out everything that Annie fancied. After all, the traumas of her brief life on the streets as a hooker, the overwhelming need for a fix without access to ZENDUST and the college course she hated, this life was great. Then suddenly, she was in a car with another South American-looking guy, except this one was younger, handsome and obviously very well educated. This guy knew the USA very well, had travelled in England and France, and had plenty of money, so, as far as Annie was concerned, he was great.

Somewhere in the recesses of her mind, Annie remembered another guy she had liked called Jonah, and she wondered what had become of him.

For the moment, Carlo Carioli was great.

He had said, "Look Annie, I know about all the troubles you went through trying to get illegal drugs, your money problems and all that stuff. Loads of people go through the same trauma all the time and there is no need for it at all. You know that. You have been getting the fixes you need and then the ZENDUST in the morning, and you are fine. Why shouldn't everyone have the same chance? The problem is that the drugs are illegal. If they were legalised, then everything would be on an even keel. They say that drugs will kill and are addictive but what about cigarettes? They kill thousands of people worldwide every day and are addictive too! Governments take a heap of tax income from tobacco; don't you think they would want to do the same with the drugs you enjoy? Of course, they would love it!! Another thing, some of the drug problem is that crackheads use stuff which is contaminated. If it was all legalised, then the problem of contaminated product would be eliminated because the makers would have to operate to good standards, like the tobacco industry. I think there will be many, many people in the world who want to see the illegal drug industry eliminated but the fact is that the demand is so great that it will never happen the way things are now. If the business were legalised, then the demand would be satisfied in a sensible way. Governments would be able to cut down on policing costs, there would be far fewer deaths from contaminated needles and such. Everyone would be free to do what they have always really fancied. It's your father and his ZENDUST we have to thank for making this new approach possible. And you, with your experience, are in the best and most unique position to spread this idea, how about it?"

"What's all this to you?" she asked.

"My company has supported and invested in your father's ZENDUST project. We believed in what he was doing and that he was a good man. Then we find out he has treated his wife so badly that she has committed suicide and he has been visiting prostitutes. We like to know and respect the people we support and your father has let us down. Not only that, but we also believe that it will never be possible to control the illegal drugs trade. There is too much demand and it's always there. Too many users die unnecessarily because of contaminated needles and drugs. We think it is better to legalise the business and ZENDUST has created that opportunity."

Carlo Carioli was a master at telling the story the way he wanted his listener to hear it. At that moment of talking to Annie, he could see his next vision coming true, the conversion of his illegal business to be wholly legitimate. What a master stroke that would be, no more problems of money laundering or arrests or harassment by the authorities!

Annie took a few days to think it all out. She had known what it was to want the fixes, to crave them, knowing that the only way to get them was via some backstreet dealer. You knew you were a criminal even then, even if you only wanted to get some stuff. The price was always outrageous and the dealer had a hold on you for dealing with him. The money had to come from somewhere, so the boys went out on burglaries, muggings and car thefts, and the girls went on the streets as hookers. It was all a dirty business but there was no stopping it, the demand was always there and always would be. Maybe the best way was as Carioli suggested, legalise it and it would be just like buying a packet of cigarettes.

"Anyway, I hate my dad for what he did to Mum. He wanted to be a saviour, like a Jesus Christ figure and look what's happened, he was out shagging hookers, ignoring Mum and me. My mum's dead because of him, she couldn't stand it any longer and killed herself. Let him see now what I can do to get my own back on him!" Her mind was made up. She told Carlo she agreed with what he said, never realising the massive worldwide furore that was about to happen as soon as the press conference was announced.

Carlo was delighted. Last time he thought that his cocaine business might be finished because of John Douglas. This time, he knew it would be the opposite and he had Douglas' daughter eating out of his hands to bring it to fruition. "I couldn't have written a better script. This could be a movie!!" he said to himself.

Annie was getting herself ready in her mindset. She had never been short of self-confidence but this was bigger than anything she had experienced before. She was very grateful to Carlo for organising everything. Even down to the stretch limo that brought her to the hotel and helped her past the media scrum.

"It's a funny thing you being here today," the make-up girl said to Annie. "I made-up your father a short while ago for his big press conference about ZENDUST. What a day that was? So many people here and he seemed such a nice man. It was terrible to hear about his wife."

Any doubts Annie had about what she was doing vanished at that moment.

Annie did the whole thing single-handed.

"Good morning, everyone," she began. She was dressed in a blue suit over a white blouse open at the neck, and with a yellow carnation in her lapel. She looked stunningly attractive and very confident in the message she had to give.

"Thank you all so much for coming to listen to me, in the exact same place where you listened to my father present the news of ZENDUST a few months ago. ZENDUST captured the interest of the whole world and we have moved on such that I have an exciting new message for you all today. First of all, you will see that I am wearing a lovely yellow carnation on my lapel.

This is my symbol of freedom and I have arranged for everyone to be given a similar carnation as you leave. These will be your symbols of the new freedom that is yours for the taking and I will now explain what I mean."

As she said these words, she touched the flower on her lapel. She knew from her teenage years that she had always had a good figure and she was savvy enough to realise that as the cameras zoomed in and as she touched the flower sitting on the swell of her bosom, the picture would be news. That introduction was a master stroke. Every TV camera and press photographer zoomed in on the flower in the lapel of this young and good-looking woman. The picture went round the globe in milliseconds. Everyone was mesmerised, fascinated and convinced that this girl had a powerful message. This was even better drama than the original launch of ZENDUST.

"I want to tell you all a little about myself and why I am here today.

"I have myself been a victim of illegal drugs," she continued, speaking slowly and looking directly at the facing cameras.

"I have been one of those sad people dealing with backstreet dealers and being exploited by them. I have been unable to pay the prices they have demanded and so I have been a prostitute on the streets to get the money they want. I have been like so many others. You in the media will have seen and reported on this kind of story many times. Too many times, in fact.

"But my message today is that it need not be like this.

"I know, you know, governments know and everyone knows now that the illegal drugs trade cannot be stopped. There is a demand from people of all ages and all walks of life to experience what the drugs offer. Certainly, some have died from the experience, but it need not have been so if the drugs had been pure and uncontaminated. The petty crimes of users are caused by the need to go to bloodsucking backstreet dealers and meet their prices. Users, just as I was, have no alternative, there is no other source of supply

"The time is now for drugs to be legalised, to be brought out of the back streets and into the real world. The danger of unrestrained addiction has been removed by ZENDUST.

"I am a living example of this new freedom. I have been able to use all manner of drugs in the evenings and ZENDUST the next morning. As you can see, I am fine and I am here to tell you that there is now no need at all for the onset of addiction. This is a new age of zero addictions, just hope, freedom and ZENDUST. This is the new freedom which my flower symbolises."

As she said these words, she touched the carnation on her lapel again, looked all around and smiled a dazzling smile that seemed to permeate the whole room. There was no doubt. Annie had the world hooked on the message she was giving.

"Legalised drugs will ensure that the prices are controlled, that manufacture is clean and standardised, and that distribution is in the high street and not in the hands of criminals. Governments will realise that they can levy taxes on the legalised products just as in the tobacco trade. In fact, the comparison with the tobacco trade is quite appropriate. Legalised drugs can and will be less dangerous that cigarettes.

"My flower is the symbol, my message is, legalise drugs, and my campaign is called the Flowering of Freedom.

"This is a moment of opportunity for all. Illegal drug users, law abiding citizens who are excluded from experiencing the highs that are available, and governments who are spending excessive amounts trying to control an uncontrollable industry. The ones who will be hit are the despicably cruel dealers, backstreet contaminators and manufacturers who don't care what they produce and sell.

"This the time for freedom from all those evil people. Let us not waste it!!"

With that ringing message, she slowly took a drink of iced water, looked around once more with her hand on the yellow flower in her lapel and sat down.

Carlo Carioli looked on from the sidelines.

"What a performance" he sighed, with a fantastic feeling of admiration and elation, "what a girl!"

John Douglas watched his daughter on TV and sighed with a terrible disappointment.

Bernado Escullos, Carlo's right-hand man at JC Investments took the microphone.

"Annie Douglas has given you all a message today, legalise the illegal drugs trade, let the people have the freedom to try what they want, without fear. Let governments be bold and grasp the opportunity to eliminate the menace arising from illegal producers and dealers.

"Annie has asked that you take this message back to your studios and newspapers.

"Later in the week, she will answer questions by appointment. Please call my office.

"Thank you all for coming, I know you will have found it worthwhile.

"Now, please pick up your yellow carnations as you leave, and wear them to remind you of Annie's mission: the Flowering of Freedom."

At that, Bernado took Annie's hand and, pausing once more to smile all around the room, they left the platform.

Chapter 20
Strong Reactions

The reactions were instantaneous and worldwide. There were some half-hearted outcries against such a foolhardy policy from a few governments, even though it was well known that some countries had legalised hard drugs before the advent of ZENDUST. In private, governments metaphorically rubbed eager hands at the revenue that hard drugs could bring into the coffers.

There was a corresponding storm of approval from young and even middle-aged folk who could not see the problems, now that the dangers of addiction had been eliminated by ZENDUST. Many of them were doing the drugs anyway but the new approach by Annie could make their habits become risk-free and possibly cheaper.

The United Nations had to hurriedly review the progress of their UNZAP programme and a security council meeting was called by China. UNZAP had been designed to deal with hardcore addicts, but this was different. China looked back into history and the times when opium was imported wholesale by British trading companies causing untold misery for millions of Chinese hooked into opium dens and their deadly pipe.

They had no wish to see any addictive drug legalised, even if ZENDUST seemed to lift the danger. The Chinese psyche has a long memory for such matters.

Police forces across the globe could see a mighty burden lifted from their shoulders if Annie's Flowering of Freedom campaign was adopted. Chasing dealers would become a thing of the past and the amount of petty crime would fall instead of rising year after year.

Carlo was anxious to see what the five narcotics families from Colombia would make of Annie's ideas. These families controlled the illegal drugs business and what they decided was crucial. Families like the Cariolis had made their money and now wanted the whole business to be legitimate and Carlo thought that Gomez would think the same. They were tired of being chased by the law. The other three principle families, would have to move into line. Furthermore, they were all investors in ZENDUST via JC Investments so had everything to gain from Annie's plan.

Carlo reflected that his decision to embrace ZENDUST and not to fight it had been a masters stroke. Worthy of his Harvard Business School training!! He also had a niggling thought in his mind as he realised that Gomez might not wish to see any more success for the Carioli family. There was unfinished business concerning Rico.

Annie Douglas was the focus of all this attention, just as her father had been when ZENDUST had been launched. She loved it, just as he had done that oh so short a time ago.

Nothing was heard from the father of ZENDUST, Dr John Douglas. DARC had kept him under wraps at the New Mexico clinic. Joe Fredericks had answered the questions about Annie's campaign on behalf of DARC with some unadulterated nonsense about "reviewing their policy on ZENDUST in due course" whereas everyone knew they couldn't have been more delighted at Annie's proposals and the way that Wall Street had marked up the share prices.

John couldn't make up his mind as he looked after his addicts at the clinic. Was Annie being completely outrageous or was she really talking good sense? Many had tried to stop the spread of drugs like crack and cocaine and none had succeeded, probably no one ever would, given the fact that there was a demand which was unstoppable. He switched from cursing the very day that Annie had come into the world to wondering whether he and Val had perhaps inadvertently created a visionary. At those moments he felt a breath of air that could have been Val whispering into his ear and he could feel tears forming at what had happened to his life and to his wife. Then, moments later, he would be blaming Annie as the main reason why he was stuck out at this clinic and blinding himself with jealousy that she was now enjoying the limelight that so recently had been his. He had tried to call Annie and had been rejected; well, so be it, he thought, let's see what happens, my addicts come first, I can help them to a ZENDUST addiction-free life.

In New York, Luke Simons, CEO of SGB, was desperately trying to fend off criticism at the monthly board meeting. The same questions were raised but much more urgently. After Annie's press conference there seemed to be a real chance that her ideas would be accepted worldwide. The same questions came up, attacking Simons over his leadership: "When will SGB's version of ZENDUST be ready? How is the testing going? Any problems? Why is our share price taking a hammering on Wall Street??

Luke Simons already hated John Douglas for inventing ZENDUST and making him and his company look like a second rate 'me-too' company rather than a leader. Now he was developing an equally strong aversion to his famous daughter. Other board members were urging him to meet Annie Douglas and take a lead in the discussion on legalising drugs and the Flowering of Freedom campaign. For Luke Simons, CEO of the world's largest pharmaceutical company, the idea of asking to meet the daughter of the man who had caused him so much grief was anathema but he caved in as the vote was taken and the board decision made. He agreed to call Annie Douglas, but he hated the idea of falling into line with the armies of junkies and crackheads demonstrating in every capital city for the adoption of Annie's proposals. To him, it looked like a rerun of the sixties, when the flower-power movement started the easy life of dope and free sex, a time when he was working hard at college to get his degree and get on in life, as he saw it

He was, however, the ultimate corporate man: what needed to be done for the company's good would be done. Luke Simon was the urbane and cultured type that you would expect to see at the head of a large corporation. He was tall, slightly greying, and fifty-seven years old. He had started at SGB straight after college. After the board meeting had broken up he went back to his office. Looking out over Manhattan, he wondered how best to approach the young and attractive looking Annie Douglas who had looked so exciting and sexy at the "Flowering of Freedom" press conference. She could have been his daughter, he mused, except his one and only try at marriage had soon ended in divorce as his wife had come to realise that his priority in life had been SGB and not her.

A formal business meeting didn't seem appropriate. So what else? Maybe he could ask her to spend a day on the company's yacht, looking for porpoises or dolphins. *That might attract her agreement,* he thought to himself. *At least she wouldn't see me as a threat to her love life, he chuckled.*

For Annie life was a dream. Everywhere she went she saw lapels emblazoned with yellow carnations.

She had decided to wait for a few days before responding to the multitude of requests from TV shows, newspapers and media barons throughout the globe. She knew she was onto a winner,and the delay enabled the momentum of the Flowering of Freedom to gather steam at an enormous rate. She didn't need to do anything to stoke the fires, they were burning anyway.

Her Flowering of Freedom campaign was unstoppable, egged on by the www.havefunwithZENDUST.com website, with its millions of hits. The media had picked up on the idea that it was an evolution of the sixties flower-power movement, mostly because those executives now running the media had been part of the sixties culture themselves.

Bernado was handling the calls, and he was astounded by the reactions. He dealt with them all himself except the day he received a call from SGB Pharmaceuticals' corporate headquarters. He realised that this was no ordinary newspaper hack, this was the real deal so he put the call through to Annie.

Annie Douglas was fully aware who SGB was and at first, she didn't want to take the call. Her father had often mentioned wanting to get SGB involved with ZENDUST, but it had never happened. What's more, she didn't want to be seen as a stooge or apologist for big pharmaceutical companies. It was a boring day though, stuck inside the hotel, and she was full of suppressed energy and excitement for the future so she picked up the phone.

"Miss Douglas," said the caller, "I am Luke Simons and I run SGB. I and my company are fully aware of the importance of the campaign you have launched through 'Flowering of Freedom'. You have the potential to touch the lives of millions of folk, in many, many countries. This is, as I am sure you must realise from the vast multitude of reactions you have stimulated across the world, a very profound responsibility. I personally know what it is like to have such responsibilities for life-giving products such as some of the pharmaceuticals my company produces. It takes a bit of getting used to believe me. I sometimes have found that a day by myself out on the company's boat looking at dolphins and birds has enabled me to think of the right way forward. I wonder if you would like to join me for a trip on Sunday. I promise not to bend your ear with any corporate sales patter!"

Annie thought for a moment. She was in fact besieged in the hotel. Every time she showed her face, a million flashbulbs went off and she was blinded by TV arc lights. She needed a day away from it all and what Simons had suggested struck a chord immediately.

"I hope we won't be alone on a boat far out at sea," she quipped.

"No, no, you would be quite safe! We have a crew to ensure that due decorum is observed by me and by our guests! How about it?"

"Can you get me out of this hotel without an army of reporters chasing us?"

"Of course, we are a big company, we have all necessary resources," he replied, smiling.

"I don't doubt it! See you on Sunday then," and she hung up.

Luke Simons held the phone for a minute and then put it back on the hook. He felt a frisson of excitement at the thought of the upcoming Sunday trip.

Chapter 21

The Day Out

On Sunday morning, Annie dressed in a pair of shorts a high-necked silk top. Discreet, she thought, and not too revealing. It was not a day for a sexy outfit. He was, after all, older than her father, this Luke Simons. She had checked him out on the SGB website and he seemed to be an OK guy, if a bit corporate but then he was the CEO! Nonetheless, she did her hair up well and wore a beautiful pair of earrings that her mother had given her for Christmas on her 18th birthday. She wanted to look good but not in any way wanton.

Promptly at nine, a girl turned up at Annie's hotel looking like her double, an exact replica of Annie herself. Annie opened the door and could hardly believe what she saw. It was the last thing she had expected.

"Good morning, Miss Douglas," the double said. "I have been sent by SGB to throw the waiting hordes off the trail. If you would like to leave by the rear exit with my driver Stephen, I will go out through the front exit and step into a limo that is waiting outside."

"OK" said Annie. "That's great! I was wondering how you would do it!"

Annie got her things together and left with the driver, going down the back elevator. Minutes later, her double swept out of the main exit of the hotel into a waiting stretch limo, ignoring the press and media, and immediately drove off towards Washington. The media went crazy: why was she going that way? Was it the White House? Cars were started and the chase was on. None of them realised it was all so futile, and the real target was well away elsewhere.

The SGB driver took her down to the marina and parked beside a beautiful yacht, with Luke Simons waiting at the quayside.

"Good morning, Miss Douglas, I see the trick worked well," he said. "Thank you for coming and welcome to our yacht! She is called *New Dawn* and I love her!"

Annie was enthralled. She had always loved the idea of sailing on a beautiful yacht into a perfect sunset. It seemed to be such a lovely, romantic and peaceful way to spend time.

"Thank you so much for inviting me. I have been a prisoner in that wretched hotel for days and this seemed a perfect opportunity to escape for a day." She smiled charmingly at Luke.

He appraised her without seeming to, as he always did with people he had just met.

"I know very well how that feels, let's get on board and away!" and with that, he took her bag in one hand, her hand in his other, and led her up the ramp, calling to the crew to let go and set sail before any of the press turned up.

The day was perfect, the wind steady but not too strong, so *New Dawn* stretched out into the bay like the thoroughbred yacht that she was. The crew handled her expertly and they sailed up towards the Connecticut and Rhode Island coasts.

Annie sat with Luke in the cockpit, and just enjoyed the sensations of slipping through the waves with only the rush of the seawater and the flap of the sails to disturb her peace. As they went out further, the dolphins appeared as if on plan, and danced around the boat in a kind of choreographed ballet of the oceans. It was wonderful. She felt that she hadn't enjoyed a peace like this for a very long time indeed and began to relax. As the waves slipped by, her mind drifted back over her life. Mum and Dad always telling her not to do things, to be careful, to pass her exams and all that jazz. She remembered getting away to college with such high hopes of the freedom that provided. The sex, apparently so wonderful before she had it, but very disappointing in reality. Messy and squalid had been her main memories. The drugs were soft at first, but they had little effect, so transitory. Then the urge came to get something stronger, and the crack-induced calm was overtaken by the recurring and overwhelming need—yes, in reality it was addiction, the absolute and desperate necessity to get another hit. Then she hadn't the cash to buy what she needed, so next came the awful experience of being out on the streets trying to sell herself for enough to go back to the dealer. All of those experiences were sensations, always just superficial sensations, which passed away and left a gap which only more of the same would satisfy. There had never been anything deeper in that life, except perhaps Jonah, but he was long gone. There was definitely a gap waiting to be filled.

The boat suddenly tilted alarmingly as the mainsail whipped back across the cabin and they turned into the wind. The motion jerked Annie out of her dream, back into the delightful reality of the day. Luke Simons took the wheel from the crew, looked across at her, and said , "This is about the only time I feel really in control of what's going on in my life." He smiled at Annie with such an air of open honesty and lack of any hidden agenda that she saw for the first time a tall and rather handsome man with a fetching touch of grey in his well brushed hair waving wildly in the wind.

"I know what you mean; my life has been out of my control since I left home" replied Annie, "there was so much I wanted to experience, so many new people to meet and things to do. In the end, it all got out of hand. I never really thought about what I was doing, all I know is that Dad was busy with his work, Mum wanted me to stay a little girl, and I wanted to be me, not the me they wanted me to be, just me. When I went to college, I knew I would have a go at drugs and all that, it meant nothing to me because I already knew that Dad had ZENDUST and so there was never any risk for me. Except it *did* get out of hand, and I was hooked too much

206

and too soon, before I could get enough of Dad's stuff, that's when I went off the rails a bit. Please stop me if I am becoming rather boring and self-obsessed, it's just that my life has not been what I wanted at all. No, no, no, not what I wanted at all"

She smiled at Luke as she realised that she had been talking as if in a dream. *"Oh my goodness, she thought, I hope he won't start to think I am a complete nutcase"*

Luke replied, "I am so different. I never went off the rails, or really wanted to, even when the flower power and heavy rock bands were so popular. I wanted to make a success in business, to be the guy that ran things, not the guy who was told what to do, where to go, when to report, and have to take all that crap. I worked hard at college, and then at business school, and then all the way up the corporate ladder at SGB. Now, as a reward, I can take the boat out on Sundays," and he laughed with pleasure as the boat sang through the swell of the waves.

Annie laughed too, enjoying sharing the moment, their feelings and their honesty together.

"Come on," he said, "you try steering the boat."

Annie stepped up to the station and took the big stainless-steel wheel in both hands.

"Hold on tight," said Luke, "these waves can knock it out of your hands if you're not careful!"

The wheel bounced and shook in her hands as the water rushed beneath the keel, but she held tight. It was exhilarating! For the first time for a long time, she was in charge, she was in control, and she felt great.

It was hard work though, and after a few minutes, Luke took the wheel from her, called the crew and said, "Let's go get some lunch."

The day flew past for Annie, and for Luke Simons. Each of them was surprised at how much they had enjoyed the day and each other's company.

As they drew near to the harbour at the end of the day, the sun was setting and scarlet rays split the azure sky, Luke turned to Annie for a moment and said, "Thank you for coming, Annie Douglas, I haven't enjoyed a day out like this for years. Of course, I know about your father and DARC and ZENDUST and I know how thrilled you must be at the reaction you are getting with your Flowering of Freedom campaign. I also know that your father set out to save lives with his work and ZENDUST, and I can see that you and your campaign have the best of motives. Just remember, sometimes what you say and the actions people take after you have said things, cost lives. People die as a result. I know, it has happened in my company when I have been in charge. It can be a terrible burden. ZENDUST has undoubtedly saved lives, just try to make sure that Flowering of Freedom doesn't cost lives."

He reflected for a moment then brightened up and said to her, "I'm sorry for the lecture, I just know the sort of things that can happen. Please forgive me."

Annie reached and took both of his hands in hers, smiled at him, and replied, "Thank you, I really need someone to help me in the situation I am in and give me some home truths. I hope I can call on you?"

"Of course, any time. Maybe another boat trip?" and he withdrew his hands from hers, although the very touch of her had quickened his heartstrings as never before. He was a little frightened by the tingling frisson of emotion that had momentarily overcome him. He really hoped she would call, and soon. He was in something of a whirl, the girl was years younger than he was, but she was stunningly attractive, easy-going, and a joy to be with. But what about the campaign she was involved with, how did that square with SGB?

The boat drew into the marina, the day was over, a day which had stirred up deep-set feelings and emotions which he hadn't felt for a long, long time.

What a great day, and a great girl he thought as she got into the car and looked back at him with a smile of pleasure and sincerity that illuminated her face. The look she gave him was filled with a depth of feeling and intensity of emotion that neither she nor he had experienced in a very long time. The message that passed between them could not then have been put into words, but both Annie Douglas and Luke Simons took the unspoken meaning with a sense that this was not the last time they would meet. Indeed, there might be a future that neither of them could at that moment explain, but which they both awaited with a mixture of trepidation and optimism.

What a day, thought Annie as she looked back, *I never really expected to like him so much.*

As the car drew away, a single flashbulb caught her eye. One enterprising reporter had waited all day for the picture of Annie Douglas, the Flowering of Freedom star, leaving Luke Simons on the SGB corporate yacht

He captured the moment and thought *how very interesting!*

Chapter 22
Matters Arising

As soon as Annie opened the door of her hotel room, the phone rang. It was Carlo.

"How did you get on with Simons?" he asked excitedly. "Did he want to know all about the campaign?"

"No, he didn't ask about the campaign at all. In fact, he was very nice and I had a good day out. That's all there was to it."

"Oh." Carlo sounded very disappointed. Annie reacted to the tone in his voice and knew that there was some sort of hidden agenda in Carlo's call. She certainly didn't want to talk about it right now whilst the memory of the day was still hot in her mind.

"I'm tired now," she said, "call me tomorrow," and put the phone down, leaving it off the hook so that no other calls would interrupt her thoughts of the day.

Annie went over the day in her mind. The trip on the SGB boat. Meeting Luke Simons and sailing that beautiful yacht together. The freedom to chat about her life and to listen to him as he talked about his. She was in a turmoil. She stripped off her clothes, ran a bath, soaked in the warm luxury of the fragrance provide by the hotel, and drifted into a reverie of peace and pleasant thoughts, contemplating Luke and what he had said about the campaign and her responsibilities if things went wrong. Every possible thing that had come up during their conversation. Annie felt she had experienced a meeting of minds that she had never found with anybody else, not her dad, nor her mum nor anyone at all that she could remember.

She went to bed soon after and drifted off into sleep wondering what it might have been like if Luke Simons had been beside her. What was he thinking in his lonely bed? … Was he wondering what it might have been like if she was in his bed? He was, after all, a lot older than she was… but was that really important…? She didn't know… or care… it had just been a wonderful day and dreams never come true… do they?

Promptly at seven o'clock the phone rang. She roused herself sleepily, "Yes?"

"This is Carlo; we have a busy day so will you be down for breakfast at eight?"

"OK," she replied and put the phone down. Remembering the day on *New Dawn* and the advice from Luke Simons, she thought, *Am I right in all this campaign?*

But that was yesterday she thought, and she resolved to get up, get showered and get on with the day. Luke Simons may have said many things but there really was no reason why the illegal dealers should continue getting away with big money on the backs of poor losers when it could all be stopped. Especially now that ZENDUST was available.

The phone rang again just as she was going into the shower, how bloody irritating.

"Yes?" she barked.

"Hello Annie, remember me? This is Jonah," said the voice from the past.

It took her a moment to recover from the surprise, and then she softened, remembering her college days.

"Of course I do. How are you? Where are you?"

"I'm in New York. I run an underground newspaper on the drug scene here in the Big Apple and the New York Addicts Anonymous Centre. We have a great interest in your campaign and what you are doing. I know all the druggies on the scene here and you seem to have so much power to do what we have been hoping for. I was so sorry when you disappeared from college and always wondered what became of you. Now I see you are on every front page, you're a star! I'm so impressed! I know you must be very busy, but can we meet up for a drink or something?"

She thought for a moment, thinking about all the people who were asking for a moment of her time. Interviews, TV shows and God knows what else, but Jonah was a voice from the past, a time when he had really aroused in her a depth of feeling, enjoyment of life, and fun when they were together. The memories were too strong to cast away.

"Of course, I'd love that. Why don't you come around here about six tonight?"

"Will do. See you later," he said and it was done.

From a life devoid of emotion and feelings, she was suddenly overloaded. What with the day out with Luke, now Jonah from her past, her dad's call, thoughts of her mother, not to mention the strange experience of being held at that ranch by that creepy, Gomez. This was the whirl in which she had suddenly found herself. She needed time to think. She would call Carlo to say she needed a break and would see him later.

At that same moment, Luke was in his office at SGB taking a call from Joe Goldstein.

"Well, how did you make out? Is she going to call off the campaign?"

"No, she is not going to call it off. In fact, we didn't really get around to that. I was able to warn her about what might happen though. It won't be all sweetness and light."

"Well, Luke, you must know that the board are very concerned about how well DARC is doing with ZENDUST, and the fact that we are not even in the game. Now, with this Annie Douglas campaign, their sales will shoot up. Another thing, we don't want to be seen to be dancing only to DARC's tune, we want to make our own music. We are ten times the size of DARC, or were in value, until they got Douglas and ZENDUST. So when will SGB's version be ready?

"You should be wary too, Luke. Get on with it, otherwise your position is going to get fragile, you know what I mean?"

Luke knew exactly what he meant. He needed to be successful, to do better than DARC, sort out the implications of Annie's campaign and soon, or else no more Luke Simons at SGB, no more boat trips on the yacht on Sundays, and then no more chances to relax with Annie Douglas. Luke knew in his heart he didn't want that to happen.

The phone broke into Annie's thoughts. All mixed up, complicated, difficult and surprisingly resonating with her heartstrings. It was Carlo again.

"Are you coming down?" He sounded irritated. Annie hadn't realised that time had slipped by as she fantasised about the times she had been with Jonah, and, by comparison, what it might be like to go to bed with someone like Luke Simons, the boss of SGB no less, very cultured and urbane, but old enough to be her father. Quite the opposite of Jonah! And what about Carlo, he was on the scene too.

"I'm on my way!" and she hurriedly did her hair and dashed out to the elevator.

Carlo's irritation vanished as soon as he saw her. He had known many women in his thirty five years but none had the fresh appeal of the Douglas girl, or the brains to see the opportunity of ZENDUST as a morning-after pill. Then to carry it all through the press conference and the launch of her own idea, the

'Flowering of Freedom' campaign, which was such an enormous success.

"Hi Annie," he said rising from his chair. "You look great!"

"Thanks, Carlo."

"Bernado has been taking that many calls about the campaign. We are definitely onto a winner here and you're the star of the show. Everyone wants to talk to you!" Carlo's enthusiasm overcame any of the doubts in Annie's mind, especially the warning that Luke Simons had given her about not being too hasty. The thought of being the star of the show put everything else out of her mind.

"OK, that's great, so where do we go from here," she asked.

"Out to dinner at Largo's for a start," replied Carlo, taking her hand.

"Great, give me ten minutes," she said, completely forgetting that Jonah was on his way.

In Medellín, Fernando Gomez continued brooding over the killing of Rico. It had been a personal pleasure watching Carlo's man Diego shot dead in front of his eyes, but he knew that the real person responsible was not Diego. It was Carlo Carioli. Killings of family members had to be avenged, they always had been and always would be, at least in the Gomez family. Rico had been the light of his life, especially as he himself was growing older and the fun of life was passing him by. He had loved the times when life had been spicy, dangerous, and full of enemies to be fooled or eliminated. Like the gringos in the USA who would never stop the drugs coming in as there were always too many people wanting them. He had loved the danger of the nightly fast boats into Miami, and the drinking and women that flowed as easily as the dollars. Life was a bore now.

Fernando Gomez spent his days brooding. Vengeance would come, the vendetta would be satisfied but not just yet. Carlo Carioli was doing a good job for the Gomez family at the moment, with this business of ZENDUST and the daughter of that man Douglas. But the time would come and he would enjoy watching the light of life fade from the black eyes of Carlo Carioli, just as it had with Diego. Fernando Gomez would be happy to die then, but not until then. Meanwhile, he walked in the beautiful gardens of his home looking over the hills and tended the roses. He saw one with a small blemish and cut off the head, thinking that it was a pity it wasn't the head of Carlo Carioli that fell to the ground. Only it wouldn't be as quick as that, Carlo would die slowly, by the hand of Fernando Gomez, whose life he had destroyed when Rico had died.

Jonah arrived promptly at six p.m., to be told that Annie Douglas was out and had left no message. The desk reception clerk didn't much like the look of Jonah, dressed as he was in jeans and an ancient sweater.

"Are you sure?" he asked at the hotel desk.

"Yes sir," and the clerk looked away to greet another guest.

"Can you give her this package?" said Jonah, trying to attract the clerk's attention again.

"OK, OK," and he took the pack and dismissed Jonah without a further look. Jonah realised that Annie's lifestyle was now very, very far away from him. Looking around at the luxury of the hotel atrium, with the whizzing glass elevators and wealthy clientele, he turned away and walked out into the night and into the subway station, back to his drug addicts.

It's a pity she wasn't there, he thought to himself as he went down the staircase into the subway hall. *Annie has done a great thing with her campaign. Some of the people I see every day think that heaven on earth has arrived with the "Flowering of Freedom." I only hope it works out for them and for Annie too.*

He had meant to tell her that he had received a visit from a representative of the UN committee investigating the whole drug business and they'd had a long talk about what needed to be done for the addicts Jonah was looking after.

The train ran noisily into the station. Men and women shouted and shoved each other aside to get in and out. Jonah was pushed out of the way and stumbled backwards; the doors shut and the train left, leaving him still on the station. He was left behind again; it was the story of his life.

Chapter 23
Rollercoaster Rolling

John Douglas turned from the TV newsreel in his room and rang the bell for his next patient at the New Mexico clinic to which he had been assigned after the incident with the hooker, the suicide of his wife, and the furore which had followed from his boss at DARC. He had always got a certain satisfaction from helping the addicts who were constantly at his door, but now all they wanted to know was how to get enough ZENDUST to enable them to keep on with the drugs they loved, but now without the dangers. Annie had set their world free, given them what they wanted, needed, craved and couldn't do without. 'Flowering of Freedom' had given them a kind of freedom, but enjoyment and the kicks they got from coke and crack and the myriad of other substances still had them trapped. The effects were always so good, the risk now eliminated, so that they had no reason or interest in giving the stuff up. It had been like that for weeks, ever since Annie's press conference in the Manhattan hotel where he, Dr John Douglas, had once held the world's press and media in the palm of his hands. How life had changed. Every time he turned on the TV news channelsit was his daughter Annie who was the star of the show and her campaign. It had really taken off, like the proverbial rollercoaster, gathering momentum and support from addicts, recreational drug takers, governments, health departments and police everywhere.

The door opened, and in walked a young guy of about thirty years, looking every bit the sharp go-getter of the business world, eager to make millions, or preferably billions, and without delay.

"Good morning; please sit down," began Douglas.

"Dr Douglas, I am not here to ask for advice on addiction. I have a business proposition for you. My name is Jed Roberts, and I represent XTech Pharmaceutical Research of New Jersey. We know that you were the driving force behind the development of ZENDUST and we, of course, also know that you have had some personal problems. We do not want to dwell on those problems, but we feel that perhaps you have had time to reflect on what happened to your wife and the incidents with hookers and are now ready to put that behind you and get back to doing what you are renowned for, brilliant and innovative pharmaceutical research. ZENDUST has taken off like a rocket, and we know that is all tied up by DARC and that majors like SGB will come out with something similar soon. We do not want to compete as a ZENDUST lookalike, we cannot do that, we want something as revolutionary as ZENDUST and we feel that you have the brains and imagination to work with us to create such a new revolution.

"Perhaps you might yourself consider that your work here is wasting your talents. Flowering of Freedom has put clinics like this practically out of business.

"You may already know something of our company,ut I have a package of information to leave with you. When you are ready, please give me a call and thank you for your time."

Jed Roberts stood up, held out his hand to shake Douglas', smiled at him, and turned abruptly, shutting the door behind him. Clearly, he was a man in a hurry; he had no time to waste.

Well, that was a surprise, thought Douglas. He pressed his buzzer to the receptionist outside.

"Hold the calls for the moment," he instructed. "How many patients are there waiting?"

"None," came the reply, "it has been like this since your daughter's Flowering of Freedom campaign hit the news."

Jed Roberts was right, clinics like this were doomed. DARC would realise that soon enough and he, John Douglas, would be dumped. ZENDUST would finish his working life.

How bizarre can life get, he mused and turned again to the TV news.

There was a news conference at the UN today and linkman was doing his intro, aware that he had an audience of millions worldwide:

"Good afternoon from ABC Newsline and welcome. Today we have a report from the UN Taskforce assigned to respond to the Flowering of Freedom campaign launched in this city by the famous Annie Douglas. The campaign has had such a massive impact worldwide that the UN has created this special taskforce to examine the possibilities of legalising the illegal trade in hardcore and addictive drugs from countries like South America and the golden triangle group in South East Asia. These countries have long campaigned that they are only responding to the demand from the developed world, such as here in the USA. They point to the fact that no campaign nor the billions of dollars that have been spent on anti-addiction programmes has ever worked. They also say that the number of deaths and the criminal and healthcare costs are the result of the fact that the drug trade is illegal and hence has created the opportunity for criminals to cash in and prey upon our young folk. The problem has always been the danger of widespread addiction but Annie Douglas has shown us a new way, with ZENDUST and the Flowering of Freedom campaign..." As he said this, he touched the yellow carnation in his buttonhole. *"... as Annie herself said,"* he reminded his audience, *"this flower is the symbol, my message is: legalise drugs.*

"We will now cut directly to the UN presentation and the chairman of the taskforce, Mr Bom Patta of Burma."

The small, slight figure of Bom Patta rose to his feet, almost hidden behind the forest of microphones. Everyone wanted to hear what he had to say.

"Ladies, gentlemen, members of the Security Council and of the United Nations, and representatives of the world's press and TV stations. I will not keep you long, we know how much satellite links for the media cost!! I have to report on our visits to the illegal drug producing nations and to the nations where the demand for illegal stimulants has given the lifeblood to this worldwide trade. On the one hand we have poor countries; on the other are the rich. The rich people want the cocaine and all the other drugs, and the poor countries, who often have nothing else, cannot see why the leaders of the rich countries want to stop them producing and selling what the citizens of the rich countries clearly desire. We know that there are some problems of uncontrollable addictions, but that is true of cigarettes, which the rich countries control through their big companies, and they allow that addiction to continue with only the token gesture of warnings on the packets of the cigarettes. We, in our group of investigators, have often considered that if the Western countries were the producers of cocaine and opium, then we would be able to buy these products on every street corner in every city and in every country, just like tobacco or whisky.

We recognise that the problems of crime and illness and deaths are the result of the fact that the trade is carried on by criminal gangs. Everyone in the world knows that the trade cannot be eliminated; the demand has grown in spite of all the campaigns such as 'Just Say No' run in Western countries. The reason is that thousands of illegal drugs are taken by mouth or smoked or injected every day, and the number of deaths is far less than those caused by smoking tobacco. Everybody knows this, so the perception is that the danger is exaggerated. The real danger is that the price, quality and purity of the drugs is uncontrolled because it is in the hands of illegal gangs and criminals."

Looking across to where Annie was sitting, he said, "We have to thank Annie Douglas and her 'Flowering of Freedom' campaign for creating the situation where the so-called 'recreational' drugs trade can be discussed openly and rationally. Never before have we had such an opportunity to bring together producers, consumers, and governments, illegal or legal, for such open discussions.

"The two key issues are that, firstly, the trade is unstoppable and that demand comes mainly from the rich countries, secondly, that the rich countries have made it illegal. We feel that the problem is not the trade, it is the illegality. It is not possible to stop the trade, but it is certainly possible to stop the illegality.

"It reminds us of the situation in the United States of America, when alcohol was made illegal and resulted in the criminal gangs of Al Capone controlling a product such as whisky for which there was an unstoppable demand. The problem was removed with the end of Prohibition.

"Likewise, if the drugs trade was legalised. Legalised production could be controlled, quality and purity would be improved. Proper channels of distribution would be established, so users would be freed from having to buy from criminal gangs, and prices would be such that the need for money from petty crime would be greatly reduced. Finally, we now know that uncontrollable addiction can be prevented by the use of ZENDUST as Annie Douglas has proposed.

"We know that countries such as China look back on their history and the effects of opium brought in by foreign traders resulting in the Opium Wars, but we would remind you again that this was the result of trading from a rich country to a poor country and enforced legality of an uncontrolled kind. We consider that we can now move ahead to a situation where such history cannot repeat itself.

"I would like to acknowledge the help and support given to this investigation in private discussions with many people in many countries, particularly Mr Carlo Carioli, Miss Annie Douglas and Mr Jonah of the New York Addicts Anonymous Centre.

"We therefore recommend to the world that the production, distribution and sale of drugs based on cocaine, heroin, opium and their derivatives should be legalised worldwide," and with that stunning announcement, Bom Patta took a drink from the glass by his lectern, looked briefly around to gauge the effects of his words, and sat down.

Annie Douglas was stunned when she thought of what had happened as a direct result of her campaign. To paraphrase some famous words of Winston Churchill she thought, *Never had so much been achieved by so few to change the lives of so many.*

Carlo Carioli, Luke Simons at SGB Pharmaceuticals, Jonah and Joey and the people at DARC, gangsters and governments, dealers and doctors, police and petty criminals, healthcare experts and economists, millions listened to the broadcast and each had their own ideas as to what came next. More riches for Carioli, DARC and the like, more challenges for Luke Simons at SGB; freedom from the law for Joey and Jonah's friends, and consequences good and bad for a rainbow coalition of others affected by what Bom Patta said that day.

For Carlo, it was the culmination of all he had hoped for and planned, now his family could legally trade his cocaine and heroin products and secondly, his control of DARC through his father's company JC Investments, ensured that every user of cocaine would become a user of ZENDUST, a double whammy of riches with no downside! Now, if he could get close to the very desirable Annie Douglas, his life would be complete.

There was one man sitting quite unmoved by anything the UN may have to say. Fernando Gomez had watched the broadcast too, sitting at his fortified house in the sunshine of Medellín. He was one of those few totally unaffected by anything this nonentity Bom Patta had said. He knew only that Carlo Carioli was a doomed man. His days were numbered, but Gomez himself would pick the day and the time. The moment when Carlo Carioli believed he had the world at his fingertips and his happiness was complete, that would be the time, thought Gomez. He had not missed the pleasure with which Carlo Carioli had greeted the girl Annie Douglas when he had let her go... perhaps that would be the moment; if Carlo were to marry her, perhaps at his wedding reception, that would be just retribution. Just as Carlo had destroyed his life when his only son Rico, who had given Fernando Gomez his greatest happiness, had been killed on the orders of Carlo Carioli. The vendetta would then be fulfilled, the revenge would be sweet and life for Fernando would be complete. Whatever else might happen did not matter. Fernando Gomez was a patient man; he would wait and continue to respond when the Carioli family consulted him on the progress of their investments in the DARC company.

George Kent and Dan Solomons watched the TV from their boardroom in New Jersey; they were amazed when they saw Carlo Carioli sitting in a prominent place as if he were a prime mover in the Flowering of Freedom campaign, and astonished when Bom Patta

227

went out of his way to thank Carioli for his efforts and effectively identify him as a representative of the South American producers of cocaine, crack, heroin and the like who had contributed to the UN investigation.

"Whoa, did you see that?" said Kent. "Is he really one of the producers? Maybe that was where all the cash had come from, by sales of cocaine and crack to fund ZENDUST?"

Solomons pursed his lips. "If he has really done that, we and DARC may be in trouble in the future for illegal money laundering in the form of an investment in our company and the funding of our expansion to cope with the demand for ZENDUST. We never really looked into where the money came from, just took it and used it. Maybe we should talk to this Carioli guy again, and quick, the last thing we need now is the SEC on our backs, just when we are about to cash in our chips."

He switched off the TV as the Bom Patta presentation finished and went over to pour a large whisky for himself, and one for George Kent.

"Time for a stiff drink, perhaps?" he asked, then went on, "I'll call Carioli tomorrow, when I've had a chance to think this whole thing out a bit more. We sure as hell don't need this kind of shit right now, if Carioli really is one of the Medellín families." He had a funny feeling that the DARC rollercoaster might just be coming off the rails.

There was another watching, from a small office in the heat of New Mexico. He was definitely interested in what Bom Patta said, but he was to be severely disappointed. Not a mention was made in the whole TV broadcast of the man who had really made it all possible, Dr John Douglas, and he watched with a mixture of extremes of annoyance, envy and resentment.

How could I have been left out in the cold? he thought. *without me, none of this would have happened. ZENDUST was my idea, and it is the keystone of all this. I should have been invited; I should be there, sitting alongside Annie.*

But no one had thought to ask him what he thought of the idea of legalising the drugs trade or Annie's 'Flowering of Freedom' campaign.

John Douglas couldn't stand the idea of being the forgotten man.

He would call Jed Roberts at XTech the next day.

The rollercoaster of change for the illegal drug business gathered yet more momentum, as if there wasn't enough already.

Chapter 24
Junketing and Jobs

The world took to the Bom Patta recommendations like a duck to water; governments quickly moved to establish systems of control and approval, exactly as they had always had for products like tobacco, alcohol and OTC pharmaceuticals.

Suddenly, businessmen invaded countries in the Golden Triangle of Asia and the formerly no-go areas of Colombia and Bolivia to search for growers of poppies and set up the chemical plants to convert the plants into the fun time drugs that now everyone wanted to try.

It was like the end of the Prohibition era of America, but on a scale a thousand, a million times bigger. The world went crazy for the new experiences, young and old alike, rich and poor, everyone wanted a fix now liberated from the fatal consequences that held them back before *ZENDUST* and Annie Douglas' campaign.

Retailers jumped on the bandwagon with drinks laced with stimulants far more powerful than whisky; it was ecstasy all round as the fun time drug called ecstasy was quickly superseded by 'super-ecs' and 'extra-ecs'.

And for every one of the new fun time drugs, a packet of ZENDUST was sold.

DARC was overwhelmed with demand and was making a fortune. They couldn't care less that John Douglas had resigned; they owned his patents and he had done what they wanted with the creation of ZENDUST. He had made George Kent and Dan Solomon's billionaires and they didn't give a damn as to where he was now. In fact, after all that business of Douglas' wife and the hookers in the hotel, they never wanted to hear of him again. The only fly in their ointment was the possibility of money laundering as a result of their association with Carioli, who had indeed emerged as one of the leading, now legitimised, producers of crack, heroin, cocaine and the whole gamut of addictive drugs. Solomons had held off calling him, whilst they waited to see if anyone else had picked up on their association, especially the SEC and the US Federal Reserve Bank, who were hot on the trail of illegal funds now that the whole business was coming to light. That thought was buried in his mind though by the fantastic demand for ZENDUST and the profits they were making. He was now a billionaire according to Wall Street, a fact which brought him immense satisfaction.

The world had gone crazy for junketing with previously illegal drugs, and the ZENDUST cure-all.

But there were some for whom it had created problems and confusion in their lives.

John Douglas sat and pondered at his XTech Pharmaceutical Research computer. He was very frustrated, he knew that XTech and Jed Roberts wanted him to come up instantly with another blockbuster like ZENDUST, but he knew he couldn't do that. ZENDUST had been the driving force of his life, and it had taken years to arrive at the right formula. Anyway, he had never done it for the money and fame, he had done it to save other bright young things from the fate that had killed David, his college friend. He could never forget David getting into soft drugs, then strong narcotics and then being unable to escape except through the deadly overdose which extinguished his life.

He looked back over his life. He had been devastated by the way his best friend had died, and that had been the whole stimulus for all his work thereafter. XTech didn't know or care about all that, they just wanted another better ZENDUST, and expected him to deliver. He was just glad to be out of DARC, and especially that clinic where he was supposed to act like he was the doctor and cure hardcore addicts, a task that was now redundant. Nobody wanted to be cured, they just wanted the fun life and ZENDUST. Even kids like Joey, his first real success, were back taking everything they could get without fear, perhaps that was all to the good? He didn't know what to think now. The perils of hard-drug addiction were now in the past, or so it seemed. Joey was making money hand over fist too, he was on TV chat shows and writing his life story, eagerly sought by editors and talk-show hosts. ZENDUST had certainly given Joey not just a *ZENDUST*, not just a resurrection from the addiction in which he had wallowed, but money and fame.

As he sat in front of the computer, assessing multiple variations on the formula of ZENDUST. John's mind also slipped back to thoughts of Annie, and further back, to Val, his wife, whom he now realised he had killed as surely as if he had pushed her in front of the truck that had killed her dog. That had exacerbated beyond reasoning the depression caused by his absence, finally to push her over the edge of despair into her suicide by overdose.

His college friend David and then his wife Val, the two people who had been closest to him, killed by overdose, and that was the reason he had been so protective with Annie, perhaps too much when she was a teenager and that was why she had been so keen to get away to college and enjoy her own freedom. Now she was the guiding light of the 'Flowering of Freedom' campaign... Life is strange, he thought. He hoped to find a way back into her life, somehow and someday soon.

Meanwhile, he tried his best to do what XTech wanted, but the inspiration and motivation had vanished into nothingness, like the lives of his wife and his best friend.

In his office looking over the New York skyline, Luke Simons at SGB was also under pressure. The board meeting had told him that they had to have an alternative to ZENDUST, and quick, or else he would be replaced.

He racked his brains, pestered his research teams and privately thought long and hard as to what to do about DARC, ZENDUST and the new situation created by Bom Patta's report. He needed an inspiration, and so far, he hadn't hit pay dirt, only a lot of half-hearted and half-baked ideas from his research teams.

We can surely do better; we are SGB, a world leader in the major league, not some generic bit-player in worldwide pharmaceuticals, he thought.

He needed some space and decided to go out on the SGB boat again at the weekend. He had loved the day when he and Annie Douglas had gone out on the boat and he asked her if she had wanted to go out with him again. He had been delighted when she had accepted.

The sun had shone again and it had been such a relief to escape from the boardroom pressures at SGB. For Annie, she was getting tired of all the pressure she was getting from the media for TV interviews, newspaper articles, personal appearances and God knows what else. As before, Annie came wearing a white open-necked shirt and blue shorts, looking attractive but not overtly sexy, just as Luke would have wanted.

After lunch at a secluded mooring just off the coast, Luke had said, "Well, Annie, you're a star now, how does it feel?"

"I'm tired, overwhelmed and fed-up," she replied honestly, "I am alone with no end of acquaintances, but no affection. My family has gone; my mother is dead and my father is consumed with jealousy now that he has been effectively fired by DARC and forgotten by the media."

She went quiet for what seemed like minutes, lost in her thoughts of what had happened to her life. She looked like a little lost girl amidst the luxury and high technology of the SGB yacht. Luke Simons was captivated by her openness, her looks, her honesty, and her vulnerability. He steadied his thoughts, to stop his imagination running away with ideas of a future involving himself and Annie Douglas, 'if only', was his line of thought, followed immediately by 'don't be stupid', so he looked and waited.

She shook her shoulders, coming back to reality, and continued:

"It's not what I wanted, I only wanted to feel that others who try illegal drugs didn't end up with the experiences that I had. You cannot understand how awful it was. Nobody can, except those who have been through the same thing. I was trapped, I had to get the next fix and the only way to get money was to let some awful repulsive man grope me and make me do things to him that were disgusting. I couldn't go out mugging old ladies or breaking into cars. You cannot possibly understand what it is like to be in such a mess that the only way forward is to let filthy men mess with your private parts. The guy who supplied what I needed turned me into a street hooker and it was truly terrible, but I had to get the next fix. He was evil, but I needed him and what he could supply. There really is no alternative if you are hooked. The relief when you get the stuff is so intense and the urge to get more when the effect fades is overwhelmingly powerful."

She paused for a few minutes, as if reliving those dreadfully exhilarating drug-related experiences, and then continued.

"My dad has done a wonderful thing with ZENDUST, but it isn't enough. People still look for a fix, and the highs that go with it, but there are still problems of after-effects and residual addiction and the need to get the money to get the drugs in the first place. It's all an illegal minefield, full of evil people preying on the young. I saw a way to stop others having to go through what I and millions of others have, and I dreamt up the Flowering of Freedom campaign. I never wanted to be on TV or to talk at places like the UN. I like Bom Patta; I think he is right in what he has said, but it is all on too big a scale and it's overwhelming me. I was so glad you called and gave me a chance to get away from it all today," and she smiled at Luke Simons with such innocence and openness that he couldn't help but feel a fluttering in his heart.

"Well," replied Luke, "I hope it won't be the last time I can do this. You must know that your campaign and the success of ZENDUST and DARC has put me in a very difficult position. My company wants me to replicate their success, and soon. If I do not, then I will be replaced and there will be no more Sunday boat trips."

"Oh God," said Annie, touching Luke's arm, "have I ruined everything for you?"

"Not yet, but I have to do something soon. I have always run this company on the basis of being better than anyone else. I cannot accept that we at SGB should simply try to copy DARC and ZENDUST. We have always been leaders, not followers. We have to think of something better."

They both sipped their drinks, gazed at the sea, lapsed into silence, and into their own thoughts.

Luke Simons was consumed with thinking about what had happened to Annie, the awful punters when she had been on the street, the suicide of her mother and envy of her father, the sustained pressure she was under now with the campaign, and her unexpressed need for genuine affection, perhaps even love. He glanced at her covertly, so pretty and unassuming, yet all the world wanted a piece of her.

Annie was distraught at what Luke Simons had told her. She knew she had ruined enough good things in her life and she couldn't stand the thought that she might be responsible for this kind man losing his job at the company he loved. Luke Simons had been the one man who had been able to give Annie breathing space by inviting her on the SGB Sunday boat trips. The man Carlo was fine, but he was pushy and made Annie nervous. She never felt entirely comfortable when she was with him. There had always been something dark about him that Annie could never penetrate; he never talked about his background or early life, only his enthusiasm about ZENDUST and especially Annie's campaign to legalise the addictive drugs. And now, it had turned out that he and his family had been producing the evil narcotics for years, it might even had been his drugs which had forced her into prostitution. No wonder he had been so keen on Annie's 'Flowering of Freedom' campaign and she now felt used and soiled by her association with the Carioli family. So much so, that she had already thought about resigning from the campaign, now it had succeeded in achieving what she had originally wanted.

Sitting in the sunshine and watching the waves drift lazily past, she thought back to the moment when she had thought of the morning-after pill. It was after she had enjoyed a really powerful fix, but the sick after-effect feelings of addiction had quickly emerged, which she knew would last until the effects of ZENDUST kicked in. It was a pity ZENDUST wasn't instant. The morning-after idea was great but it still involved some of the sustained bad effects of the narcotic before ZENDUST worked its magic.

Surely if she could help Luke and his research team at SGB to look at that, then they would have something better than ZENDUST. He was a good man; what could she think of to help him, after all he had done for her?

The day was so dreamy, the sea so soporific, as if time stood still, that thoughts could wander to realms quite unreachable by conscious processes. She was very sensitive to the man standing near to her, his needs to deliver in his business, his masculinity, the unexpressed void in his life that a woman could satisfy, and the opportunity she might have to play a part in helping him to fulfilment in all of these areas.

Thoughts take flight at such moments.

All of a sudden, she had it, the key, the solution, the cure to this man's worries, all in one flash of inspiration! What if they could combine the good things of ZENDUST with the thrill of the drugs, in one pill, wouldn't that be marvellous? No need to worry about the morning after, it would be a one-time shot with fun and no after-effects at all!

She jumped up and threw her arms around him, with such excitement and happiness on her face that he wondered what on earth had happened to the pensive girl he had observed a few moments ago.

"Hey, hey! What's up? Are you OK?"

He stepped back, holding her but pushing her back to arm's length to see her face, she so excited and happy, he inwardly thrilling at the first moments of physical contact he had experienced with this fascinating girl. That momentary contact between his body and the clinging arms, firm breasts and hips of the girl Annie ignited feelings in him which he hadn't experienced for years.

"I have it," she said through her tears of joy at being able to do something for him, unaware that her clinging arms and entwined body had already done something for Luke that no one else could have done.

"I have what you are looking for, I have just thought of it, and you will be able to give SGB the lead that you want."

"What is it? What have you thought of? Come on, tell me! Don't keep me in suspense!"

He held on to her, unwilling to let her go but willing her with all his heart and soul to tell him what she had thought.

"You know that I told you that ZENDUST was OK but you still had to experience some of the bad after-effects of the narcotics before ZENDUST's therapy kicked in? Everybody wants the thrill and feelings that the drugs give, and nobody wants the bad effects but they go with the territory, so to speak; you can't have one without the other. That's how I thought of the morning-after idea, to give everyone the freedom to have the thrills but without the danger of becoming addicts. That's OK, but it isn't enough, there is still a risk if people don't bother with the ZENDUST until it is too late, then they have to go on a cold-turkey ZENDUST-only regime as my dad originally thought of when he was working on ZENDUST and looking particularly at hardcore addicts.

So, the problem for fun users is having to take two separate pills. Well then, why not take away that problem and give them a one-shot pill with plenty of narcotic to give loads of thrill and include enough delayed-action ZENDUST to kill any addictive tendency or unpleasant after-effects. Everything all included!"

Luke looked at Annie more closely than ever before, astounded, amazed and thrilled simultaneously at the idea she had shared and the feeling of having her close to him... he could scarcely speak.

In turn, she looked him in the eyes, waiting to hear his reaction, hoping against hope to be of value to him and the giant SGB company, which was his life, wondering why he didn't say anything, wanting desperately to know if he thought she was stupid and her ideas worthless, just a silly junkie's fancies... anything, just say something, please Luke...

"Annie Douglas, you are a marvel! How is it I can have teams of graduates and scientists working on how to come up with something better that ZENDUST and giving me nothing, and I have one afternoon on the boat with you and wham! There it is! You are wonderful! You have it exactly, the no-kill thrill pill; it's great, all we have to do is figure out how to do it, and if we can't with all the resources of SGB, then it's probably impossible."

"I think this deserves a celebration."

He rang the bell and one of the boat's staff appeared immediately. Luke said something in his ear and he vanished to reappear moments later with a bottle of champagne in a silver ice-bucket and two iced glasses.

Luke took the bottle from him, expertly flipped the cork, which exploded with a loud bang, shooting away out over the sea, and let the champagne bubble out into the two glasses. He offered one to Annie, picked up his own and clinked the two glasses together, saying, "Annie Douglas, you are an inspiration; thank you for being with me today; indeed, thank you for just being you," with that toast he entwined his arm with Annie's in the time-honoured fashion, and they both brought the glasses to their lips and savoured an extraordinary moment in each of their lives.

He stepped back then, with a serious look on his face, he added, "Now then Annie, let me be straight with you, you have just come up with the most ingenious solution, one which no one else has yet thought of. This idea of yours could make you rich, without me or anyone else. You just have to take the idea to any of the big pharmaceutical corporations and they will snatch your hand off. The next step is up to you.

"I have loved having you on board the boat. Every minute in your company has been like a tonic to me, but you need not feel you owe me or my company anything. If you want to go out and talk to the big multinationals then as far as I am concerned, it was your idea to do with whatever you want."

He took her glass from her and set it down, then he took both of her hands in his, and looked deep into her eyes, with a penetrating look so full of hope and innocent affection that she felt it reach to her very core.

"Annie Douglas, I would like you to know though, that if you should find it in your heart to partner me and my company in the big adventure that your idea will stimulate, then nothing and no one could make me a happier man."

He held her hands tightly and waited with bated breath for her answer. Her decision, he knew, would affect the rest of his life, his personal life as well as at SGB Pharmaceuticals Inc. He hoped and prayed inwardly.

Annie didn't hesitate, she melted into his arms, "Nothing would make me happier. I'd love to partner you," and she kissed him lightly on the lips to seal the bond between them.

He thrilled at the kiss, knowing that it signified the bond for the business, realising too that Annie Douglas meant much, much more to him than the salvation of his position at SGB; this could be a state of Zen for him too.

How strange that ZENDUST was bringing Zen to so many unexpected places, even to me, mused Luke Simons.

Chapter 25
Market Forces

Now that the growing of poppies and the extraction of mind-blowing narcotics was legal, everyone was at it. Every spare space in the traditional areas of Asia and South America was converted into poppy growing. Since the USA and Europe had been the lifeblood of the previously illegal narcotics business, everyone there was also madly growing hash plants and desperately trying to cultivate the right sort of poppies. A whole new business sprang up overnight with kits telling the innocent how to grow the plants, dry the leaves, mix the chemicals and distil the concoction into every kind of hallucinogenic creation.

The demand for ZENDUST expanded proportionally, and with it, all kinds of fake and cheapskate versions flooded in from the usual makers of counterfeit Viagra that were completely devoid of the beneficial effects of the genuine article. Users quickly found out when they had taken the fake stuff, the pangs of addiction struck immediately and they all rushed to buy the genuine product, which was all to the good of DARC and their investors, the Carioli family, and the other partners like the Gomez family who were associates of JC Investments Inc.

Carlo Carioli sat with his father and looked at the figures of income from their decision to take the families into the DARC business and ZENDUST.

"You have done well," said Juan, "but be aware that some of our partners are not happy; they feel they are losing control. There is too much at stake with DARC and the new situation we have with the Bom Patta report and all that has happened since then. Be wary, my son, there is danger."

"I know."

"Perhaps, my son, you do not really know. Our families have all grown up with danger, deaths mayhem and removing people if they cause problems. Take care. Some of our long-time friends still think the old ways are better than your new ways."

Carlo listened to his father with growing irritation. "Surely, they should look at the results from DARC, money was flowing in! What would have happened to them all if they hadn't got involved in ZENDUST and DARC!! They should all be very happy with the way we have shown, not thinking about the old days, and the old ways of killing and firebombing and all that. This is not the old days, since ZENDUST and the Bom Patta report, everything has changed and the families had better get used to it. It will never be the same again."

"Be calm, my son. Let us wait and see how they think when we next meet with the families."

Fernando Gomez had certainly been thinking. He had allowed his mental vendetta over the death of his son Rico to mature into a steady, unmitigated and deadly hatred of Carlo Carioli, the son of his long-time friend Juan. The partners in the DARC investment through the JC Investments company sometimes met to share out the proceeds and Gomez had no intention of letting the acquisition of the money interfere with his long-term plan to kill Carlo.

As usual, the families met in the offices of JC Investments in the Cayman Islands. The son, Carlo, took the chair nowadays, as Juan, Fernando and most of the others were growing old and were content to let the young man run the business so long as the profits were substantial and shared out equitably.

Carlo looked immaculate, as usual, the archetypal product of business school. Fernando Gomez, sitting at the opposite end of the table, examined him with gimlet eyes much as a scorpion would examine a prey in the moments before injecting the fatal venom with an arcing deadly stab.

"As you can see, our decision to invest in the ZENDUST anti-addiction drug and in the American DARC company has proved to be a very wise decision, and my father and I thank you all for agreeing to such a difficult decision when there was a possibility that our normal trade in narcotics might be eliminated," and he looked to his father for support. The older man nodded and smiled; he was very proud of his son, and what he had achieved by going to Harvard Business School and taking the illegal drugs business into new ways of thinking, well beyond the older methods of murder and high-speed nightly trips into Miami.

Fernando Gomez watched the older Carioli smile at his son and look so happy, thinking that when his vendetta is satisfied, then Juan Carioli will know just how he, Fernando Gomez, feels at the killing of his only son. The waiting and anticipation only added to Gomez's sure knowledge that the final outcome of the death of Carlo Carioli would be extremely enjoyable.

Carlo continued, "However, markets have changed and market forces must make us change. It will never be the same again for any of us. I am sure you will all have noticed that the demand for our production of narcotics is falling because there are so many competitors coming into the business, now that it is legal and there are not the threats that we all experienced in past times. The campaign run by the daughter of the man Douglas who started it all off with ZENDUST has come so far that legalisation has meant much more demand but also far more production and prices are falling. For us, it means that we should look to a time when we cannot compete in narcotics. We could run things profitably when we had high prices to pay off all the police, justice departments, dealers and the like, but now things are very different and our costs are too high. In the future, we will see that our best income will come from our business links with the American company DARC and the ZENDUST anti-narcotic."

Carlo knew very well that this news would sit badly with the families. They would blame him for ever allowing ZENDUST to have a life of its own. Many of those present thought he should have killed Dr Douglas years ago and have done with it. Then he had had the gall to support the Douglas girl's campaign and even sit on the UN's committee with that jerk Bom Patta.

He had much to answer for, in the eyes of the families.

"We are, as you see, still achieving a net income far higher than we would have with illegal narcotics and one day, someone would have done what Douglas and the Bom Patta committee have done. We have been very astute in ensuring that we have invested in the cure, i.e. ZENDUST, as well as in the original products, the narcotics with which we created such a demand and made so much money."

Juan Carioli nodded his agreement with his son's conclusions.

Around the table though, the feelings were very different as they pondered the implications of what had been said. To most of them, the news was bad. Many saw Carlo Carioli as the betrayer of the business that had been so good to them, their sons and daughters, their workers, dealers and collaborators.

Now, if their usual narcotics business failed, they would all be entirely in the hands of the American

DARC company and the loss of their independence was something that none of those present wished to allow.

Perhaps, the unspoken thoughts ran round the table, *We should have killed Carlo Carioli and all the Douglas family.*

Multiple murder was in the air.

Gomez was the first to voice the opinions of the other families.

Looking at the older Carioli, he said, "I will remind everyone here of what I said at the first meeting when we decided to do as your son proposed. I said that this idea of Carlo's had better work. That was the idea of getting involved with ZENDUST. I and my family have a very good business now and we feed many, many addicts who want what we have, with big profits to us. If there are problems in the future with your plan," — emphasising the word 'your' — "I and my family will do whatever is necessary to keep our business going well. Whatever is necessary," he repeated, "including eliminating people who are a threat to me, my family and our business, and that might mean this character Douglas, or his family or even you and your family if you stand in my way. That might look like a return to the bad old days to you, Carlo Carioli, but those methods have worked well for me and for my family for many years. We will be watching you closely to see how things go and we will take action if things seem to be going wrong.

"We will not see our money lost in some new plan such as you have proposed if things go badly. I said then that we will do whatever is best for our family.

"These words are exactly what I said then, at the beginning.

"It seems to me that things have not gone as my family would wish," Gomez stared coldly at Carlo, "and I do not wish to be dependent on some American company for my family's future. As you all know," he said looking around the table, "this plan has already cost me something which was dearer to me than anything, namely the life of my son, Rico. Such a loss cannot go unpunished, and I do not plan to put myself and my family in a position of dependence on the Americans.

"For instance, what plans do you have, Carlo Carioli, for the possibility that the American company will cheat us, or refuse to pay what it owes, or reneges on the deal in some way?"

"What if some other company comes up with a competitor to ZENDUST? Then, all our income will disappear as we will have no narcotics business either according to your idea."

Carlo struggled to come up with answers that satisfied Gomez or any of the other families.

He could only say that things had gone well with DARC so far and they had no reason to doubt that the arrangement would be OK in the future. Carlo knew very well that the US SEC authorities were investigating DARC for using illegal funds in their business, and those funds had come from the families sitting around the table and their illegal drugs businesses. He dared not mention that at the meeting; in fact, he had not even told his father.

Carlo told them that no other company had an alternative to ZENDUST and he knew that DARC had protection through patents and intellectual property.

Gomez sneered at this, "Patents, intellectual property! What is this nonsense! My family was never dependent on patents, we were strong in ourselves, we did not depend on bits of paper. Is this what we can expect from the Carlo plan? Dependence on bits of paper and the Americans?"

He looked around at the other families, and announced, "My family will go its own way, and my son will be avenged," and with that he got up, stared death at Carlo Carioli, and walked out.

After a few moments, all the other families joined Gomez and walked out too, leaving the Carioli father and son with their agreement in tatters and their lives in jeopardy.

Carlo looked at his father, "So be it," he said, "we will be better doing our own business without having agreement from the Gomez family or any of the others."

Juan Carioli was not so sure. He and the families had been friends for many years; it was not so easy to break those bonds.

The phone rang, loudly and insistently, breaking into the silence that had descended on Juan Carioli and his son. It was DARC.

Carlo picked it up on the open line so his father could hear. He was expecting more good news on profits.

"Mr Carioli, this is Mr Solomons from DARC. We have received a call from the US authorities regarding the financial input your company has been making to ours. We and the SEC have seen your appearances on the UN Bom Patta committee where it seems clear that you and your associates are, or were, actually producers of illegal narcotics and so the money we have received has been laundered drug money. This is very serious indeed; if the news gets out, then God knows what will happen. We could have our license for ZENDUST taken away. Why didn't you tell us where the money came from when we first met?"

"You didn't ask. You were happy to take the money on the arrangement we offered. It is not our problem."

"Yes, it is. If the SEC take us to court then all the money you get from our profits will stop. Immediately.

"One other thing," continued Solomons, "you should know that the market is being flooded with cheap copies of ZENDUST from the Far East. We can't stop it, either and their counterfeits are damned good. In fact, it's almost impossible to tell what is ours and what is a copy. It's just like the trouble the makers of Viagra had with copies, a fucking nightmare. We need to meet."

Carlo looked at his father, who was sitting and listening intently to all this. He nodded, and Carlo replied, "Yes, fine; will you come here? If there is a problem with laundered money then we do not wish to enter the United States."

"We will be there on Monday," he replied and the phone went dead.

Juan Carioli, patriarch of the family, looked at his son and said quietly, "You must be careful. Do not let Fernando Gomez know about this trouble. Deal with the people from DARC and do not admit anything about the money."

Carlo looked at his father and had the feeling that the good life for the Carioli family was about to end.

Fuck that, thought Carlo as he drained a slug of fine whisky. *I'll fix it somehow. Maybe I'll get that girl again or even that fucker who invented ZENDUST. I will not let my father and our family down. I got us into this fix, I'll get us out of it. The Carioli family has always survived, and we will again!* Pouring another large whisky, he set to figuring out his next move, just as he had been taught at Harvard.

CHAPTER 26
Annie's Personal Lockdown

In New York, Luke and Annie spent the weekend in his Manhattan apartment, making love and thinking about the possibilities that lay ahead for them both.

As she lay there, looking at Luke, Annie thought of her mother and the tragic consequences that ZENDUST had brought to the family, and of her father stuck away somewhere, she knew not where.

She knew too that she was not free of the Carioli family and remembered that terrible moment when Rico had been stabbed to death in front of her eyes in the car, what a long time ago that seemed now. She would have to tell Luke about it all sometime, but not now when life was just about perfect.

She studied Luke as he lay there, looking so peaceful in the moment but she could see, buzzing inside, alive with excitement at the future. He was fair-haired and handsome in a rugged sort of way, unthreatening, very different from the rather menacing characters she had met when she had been abducted by the Gomez family and that Carlo Carioli.

Leaning over, she kissed him, saying, "Wake up, Mr Executive, you shouldn't be lying in bed like that when there's work to be done!"

Luke was unwilling to move, enjoying the intimacy and the kiss, but his internal 'Mr Executive' took over and, rousing himself, he put on his gown and looked around for his laptop and the coffee pot.

"Right, Mistress Annie, where should we start? We need to keep this to ourselves, we don't want to let the news of your brilliant new idea leak out and then be besieged by the TV and the press, as happened last time with the launch of ZENDUST.

"Priority one: we must keep you safe, Annie. There are very powerful people about who would love to get you on their side, or even to get rid of you altogether. Maybe you should stay here in my apartment; I don't think anyone knows you are here. Did you tell anyone?"

Thinking slowly, she said, "No, I can't remember telling anyone."

"Good. I will organise security using the team we have at SGB. They will be discreet but it's important that you don't take any risks, Annie. They are a very effective team of guys and will be told not to bother you unnecessarily. They will answer the door; you should never do that yourself at the moment."

Annie was beginning to feel really scared as Luke talked on. She had just launched into her Flowering of Freedom campaign and the new website www.FloweringofFreedom.com, which was getting thousands of hits every hour worldwide. She didn't want to just disappear from the face of the earth.

"Luke, I cannot stay trapped in here. I've got so much on my plate. I have to speak at the UN and to Bom Patta about the legalisation issues. I will take care. Maybe you could get your security guys to accompany me as guards so that I can go out?"

"OK, Annie. Will you stay until I get the team here? It should only take a couple of hours. They will give you a secure text to say they are on their way. OK, stay safe, I have to get to the office and talk about our joint initiative to the board. I can't wait to tell them. It's a real new challenge for me! See you later this evening."

He dressed quickly, kissed her deeply and went out to his waiting car.

He called the Joe, the boss of the SGB security detail as soon as he was in the car and told them to get to the apartment and protect Annie Douglas pronto. "Get on the case immediately," he told them. "She is vulnerable, pretty and very important to the company, and to me personally."

Joe Slint caught the tone of Luke's voice and recognised the urgency. "We'll be there within the hour."

"I told her to expect a text from you prior to arrival, so be sure to do that for her security, Joe."

"Roger. It will be done," he said as he called his team to get their weapons and equipment for a long stake-out at Luke's place.

Satisfied that Annie should be safe in his apartment, Luke sat back and called his office.

"Hi Ginny, I'm on my way now. Get my development team ready for a briefing later but get the Chairman to make time for me as soon as I get there. I have something which cannot wait." Ginny, his blonde secretary, got the hint of something big in the offing and replied, "OK, I've got it Luke, I will fix everything" and killed the line. *I wonder what Luke is up to now,* she mused. *I hope it's nothing to do with that girl Annie Douglas he has entertained on the SGB yacht, and that stuff ZENDUST that's all over the news.* She picked up her desk mirror and made sure that when Luke turned up, she was looking as desirable as possible. She certainly wasn't going to give up her target man for this Annie. Then she did as Luke had instructed her.

Her phone lit up again.

"Hi Ginny, Joe Slint here, just to let you know we have been called to an urgent assignment at Luke's apartment to guard a girl called Annie Douglas, who seems to be very important to Luke. We'll be there with a full team within the hour. You can contact me there. OK?"

So that's it, Ginny thought.

Annie got the coffee pot boiling and stood looking out of the window towards where the twin towers had stood all those years ago. They had symbolised the overwhelming faith in the future of the American nation that its peoples had enjoyed back in 2001. Her dad, John

Douglas, had developed ZENDUST with similar faith in the future. As she contemplated all that happened to her, the release from the strictures of home, getting away to college, the freedom, trying everything, then getting into real trouble and having to get money for drugs by prostituting her own body. Then that curious episode of being taken away, suddenly released and finding the freedom to build her own way in life with her 'Flowering of Freedom' campaign and www.FloweringofFreedom.com. Annie had finally found her own hidden self.

For a moment, she had this awful feeling inside her that her campaigns and ZENDUST might be heading for the same human disaster that had befallen the Twin Towers.

Pulling herself from black thoughts, she looked again and could see the new One World Trade Centre building rising from the ashes of 9/11 entombed in the Memorial Garden. This was now called the 'Freedom Building', and Annie was inspired by the thought that this new name symbolising faith in the future would be a model for her own new life of personal freedom.

Annie couldn't stand the idea that she was about to be enfolded into the corporate life of SGB Pharmaceuticals and have her freedom stifled just as she had found it.

She hadn't heard from her dad for a while, she had been so busy. Still looking at the skyline of Manhattan, Annie wondered where he was and what he would be thinking about her campaigns. The more she thought about it, the more it began to seem that her campaigns were directly opposite to what her dad had striven for. She, Annie Douglas, was making drug taking easy, everyone could do it, John Douglas was intent on removing addicts from an early death by contaminated needle.

Annie knew now what her dad knew. There was no easy path to Zen.

Her phone rang with its shrill tone.

"Is that Miss Annie Douglas? This is the office of Bom Patta at the UN."

"Yes," replied Annie.

"Miss Douglas, we and the whole community of nations represented by the United Nations, believe that the development of ZENDUST by your father Dr John Douglas is one of the most wonderful contributions to world health of this decade. It is our intention to invite Dr Douglas to a special presentation in his honour in New York at the earliest opportunity. We are having difficulty in contacting Dr Douglas, perhaps you could contact him on our behalf?"

Annie was completely gobsmacked by the call from Bom Patta. Absolutely thrilled. *Whatever our problems,* she thought, *I am totally thrilled for Dad. I must try to contact him with this news.* He had always fancied a Nobel Prize, but this was going to be much more special. A private reception at the UN in New York, *Whoa! He'll be over the moon!! A much better fix for him than any illegal drug confection!* she smiled at this rather bizarre notion that had suddenly come into her head.

The SGB security team hadn't arrived yet, so she had a chance to call that DARC company without Luke knowing and try to locate her dad.

Picking up the phone she called DARC, and connected to their messaging service:

"Hi, this is Dan Solomons, you have reached the offices of the Drug Addiction Research Charity, sponsors of the new anti-addiction treatment ZENDUST. We are very busy so please leave your contact details and we will respond as soon as we can."

Annie spoke carefully, not wanting to give away too much information to DARC, whom she did not trust, "This is Annie Douglas; I have an urgent message for my father Dr John Douglas, who is working for DARC in one of your facilities. Please have him contact me directly. Thank you."

At the that moment, her cellphone rang for an incoming message.

"This is Joe Slint, SGB Security, I believe you are expecting me. Please acknowledge immediately."

That was it. Annie was trapped, there was nothing she could do at the moment.

Acknowledging the message, she waited for the doorbell to ring.

"Good morning, Miss Douglas, my name is Joe Slint, Head of SGB Security. We have been tasked to keep you safe and protect you from unwanted callers, press, media or any other individuals who might be a risk to you personally, or to the interest in you that we have as a company. I understand Mr Simons has briefed you about our presence?"

Joe's team began to settle in, just as if they were Annie's parents!

Taking exception to their casually dominating manner, Annie said, "Yes, he did, but I am not happy with the really intrusive way you have gone about your task. It seems overwhelming and very restrictive for me. I'll call Luke now."

Picking up her cellphone, she waited for Luke to answer. Instead, she got that sexy tart Ginny who always seemed to be making a play for Luke.

"Mr Simons' office, can I help you?"

"This is Annie Douglas. Ask Luke to call me back immediately!"

"I'm sorry, he is in a meeting right now. I'll relay your message."

"Just do that!" said Annie through gritted teeth.

She felt herself being forced mentally back into a little shell of obedience to routines, orders and the opinions of others, just as she had felt at home years ago. "I will break out," she decided, "just like before. When I get the chance!"

"Stay out of my way, Mr Slint, just call me if Mr Simons phones, and I am expecting a call about my father, Dr Douglas. It might come from the DARC company with some information, about his whereabouts."

Joe Slint replied, "We have been instructed to take any calls on your behalf, so I will inform you as to who called and any messages."

"What! I'm not to be able to answer my own phone! Well fuck you!!," and with that she stalked out of the living room, went into the bedroom which still smelt annoyingly of Luke, and worked off her anger in a fit of tears.

"I need to get another cellphone," she muttered. This would be her priority now, and quick.

But how am I going to be able to do that with these SGB goons following me round like tomcats on heat? Who do I know to fix this? That's it, Joey will be the kid who knows all about getting mobile phones, legal or not, I really don't care!"

Putting on her best face, gritting her teeth and smiling encouragingly towards Joe Slint, she returned to the living room.

"I apologise to you Joe, and your team here, for my rude outburst just then. I know that you are here to protect me. Please forgive me."

"That's OK, Miss Douglas; people often find it very strange to suddenly be subject to close protection, so no surprise to us the way you reacted. Forget it!"

"Great," replied Annie. "Just one thing, I promised to speak to one of Dad's best patients called Joey Jones, to ask him about his experiences of ZENDUST. I'll give you the number so you can keep your record of my calls. Just call him and put it through to the bedroom please?"

"OK, Miss Douglas. Will do."

"Maybe you could let me meet him in a diner just around the corner? At least I wouldn't be stuck in here 24/7. I'm sure Luke won't mind if you send someone to be there too!" She smiled sweetly at Joe.

"OK, OK, I got the message. I'll call your friend right now."

Chapter 27

Denouement Day

Dan Solomons had had a bad weekend. A few weeks ago he had been counting his net worth in the billions as the stock price of DARC had rocketed upwards. Now the whole edifice seemed to be at risk. There was that call from JC Investments and that shady character Carioli which seemed to indicate that their money had been laundered from illegal drug sales seemingly recycled as funds to support ZENDUST. He knew that would spook Wall Street if that juicy bit of news got out.

Then there had been that daft moralising UN press conference by Bom Patta talking about legalising the whole hard-drugs business. Solomons knew that would have the effect of taking control of ZENDUST away from DARC. Not to mention the idea that someone else was bound to follow Douglas' idea and get a replacement for ZENDUST. The price would collapse, along with DARC's share price.

Thank God that idiot Bom Patta hadn't mentioned the name of John Douglas. They would need to keep him locked away, especially after that incident with the call girl. That definitely wouldn't go down well with the UN.

As he got out of the elevator in his new office on the 50th floor of the new One World Trade Centre Building, he thought to himself that he rather liked the idea of an office in the Freedom Building on the old Twin Towers site.

"We've brought freedom to millions by ZENDUST," he said to himself.

At that same moment, he didn't realise that Annie Douglas was looking directly into the Freedom Building with the same sort of feelings.

The phone was already going crazy as he arrived. "OK, I'll take the messages first," he said to Julie, his secretary. Julie was anything but glamorous, but very efficient and didn't miss a trick on his behalf. Solomons had learnt long ago to keep sexy girls out of his workdays; they were a constant source of trouble.

"Good morning, Mr Solomons. There was a priority call from Annie Douglas who wants to contact her father. Bom Patta's office called, they want to speak to you and Dr Douglas about making some sort of a special UN award to recognise the wonderful outcome of the ZENDUST project. I said you would call back later today."

Collapsing into his chair, he thought, *Oh my God, what a start to the week. How do I manage this one?*

"Do you want me to make your day complete for you now, Mr Solomons? Take a look at this!"

Julie produced a copy of the day's *Wall Street Journal*, with banner headlines all over the front page:

"ZENDUST manufacturing funded by laundered cash from Colombian cartels."

"You're right, Julie, that's just about made my day and cooked my goose. Fix me a large whisky, honey. I have to think this out."

"Give me five minutes and then call George Kent." George was the President of the Drug Addiction Research Charity. Dan Solomons knew that Kent would go nuts over these headlines.

"Call the research facility where we have Douglas tucked away and tell them to keep Douglas locked up and incognito. Don't tell anyone from the press or media that you've got him. Don't tell Douglas anything. Keep him busy with the lab work. I'll call again later. OK. Got all that Julie?"

"What to do with Douglas is top of the agenda," he said to himself as he downed the whisky. Solomons didn't usually drink whisky so early in the day, but today was shaping up to be a real crisis. "Talk about the shit hitting the fan, it just did. We can't keep Douglas locked up, what with this stuff from the UN and Bom Patta. They want to give him an award and if we didn't have this news today from the *Wall Street Journal* we could have cashed in big-time with free publicity, he thought

Julie picked up as Dan's private line blinked.

"Good morning, Mr Kent. Yes, Dan is here. I'll pass you over!" and she handed over the phone like it was a ticking bomb.

Kent didn't hold back. "Dan. I've seen the headlines. What a fucking mess you have got us into. We had everything looking great and it was your idea to get involved with those Colombian cartels. Your position here in DARC is untenable.I need to save the company, our reputation, and the future of ZENDUST with us, no one else. You're going to have to take the can. The shit has hit the fan, and it's your shit, your fault. You're fired, Dan. I'm instructing Julie to see that you leave the office immediately before the press get here and you can fuck things up even more. Pass the phone to Julie and leave the DARC premises immediately."

Once he was back on the line with Julie, he said, "Julie, Mr Solomons is quitting DARC with immediate effect. Make sure he goes now, before the media pack arrive. He is to take nothing. No files, nothing, no company phone, nothing at all. When he's gone call me!" and the phone clicked dead.

Julie was traumatised. She had worked for Dan Solomons for years and couldn't believe what had just happened.

She was the one to collapse in the chair this time.

"Maybe we both need a large whisky," was all Dan could say. He had been fired; everything had gone to hell, and he was getting the blame. He had been the one at DARC who had encouraged Douglas and now he was being dumped. Douglas was going to get an award at the UN. Kent was going to make a mint of money, and he was being trashed.

"What a fucking nightmare!"

"So, is that really it, Mr Solomons, are you fired?

"Yes, Julie, I've had it here. Kent just fired me."

"Yes, Mr Kent told me, and he told me that you are to leave immediately, before anyone from the press arrives."

"Well, as of now, I don't give a shit about this place. I am off out to the wild blue yonder, whatever that might be. I'm sorry to leave you, Julie; you have been great over the years. I wish you luck with George Kent."

With that, he picked up his coat and went out slamming the door and down in the elevator, just as he had come up a few minutes ago, when he had been a Vice President of DARC. Now he was on the way down, literally.

Julie sat and downed the whisky. The phone went again "Hi Julie, has he gone? Did he go quietly?"

"Yes, Mr Kent, just as you ordered. What can I do for you now?"

Just then, Julie saw an email arriving from the UN *"FAO: DARC Inc. We have seen this morning's announcement concerning the origin of funds used to commercialise ZENDUST. Clearly, we cannot continue with the discussions about a special presentation to Dr Douglas at the moment, although we reserve the right to make an award when he is shown to be separate from any links DARC may have had with illegal drug cartels. From the Office of Mr Bom Patta, Secretary General, United Nations, New York."*

"Oh my God. Wait till Mr Kent sees this!"

Kent's world was disintegrating before his eyes and in real time. DARC's stock price was plummeting downwards; he was moving from being a billionaire to millionaire to poverty in minutes. The phone rang again, it was non-stop today.

Annie had got Joey to give her a phone when they had met at the diner. Joe Slint never saw how Joey did it, he was good at that sort of trickery.

"Hi! Is that the DARC office? My name is Annie Douglas, my father is Dr Douglas who has worked with you on ZENDUST. I really need to contact him. You must tell me his number or get him to call me immediately. Can you do that?"

Julie knew that Annie and Dr Douglas must know about the news this morning, and she sounded in a terrible state. Dan Solomons was gone so whatever orders he had given Julie earlier were history, so she took pity on Annie and texted the contact numbers she wanted.

George Kent was shattered by the events of the morning, but he was not a man to give up quite so easily. He had come from a hard schooling in business. Thinking aloud, he said, "How to get out of this godawful mess?" as he poured another large whisky. "The problem is the connection with that crowd at JC Investments, especially that young guy Carlo, and getting Douglas back on board. We need the money but we don't want them, so who else is there? JC they have turned into total poison. We need Douglas for his PR value. I'll call him and explain that Solomons was the guy who sent him away and behaved like shit."

Julie had just called and told him about the message from Annie, and that she had told Annie where to find her dad.

That's just great, he thought, *it'll show Annie and Douglas that we want them to be back together as soon as possible. At least that will fix the Douglas problem for the moment!"*

His personal phone rang: "Yes, Kent here, who is it? I'm very busy; this had better be urgent!"

"Mr Kent, my name is Luke Simons, Executive Vice President at SGB Pharmaceuticals, we spoke once before about collaboration when you were launching ZENDUST. You turned us down then, but I have a feeling you might not turn us down this time."

Kent reacted quickly, thinking, *Oh, my God, salvation is at hand!*

Speaking carefully so as not to give away too much, he said, "What did you have in mind?"

"I'll be blunt, Mr Kent. You know, and I know that DARC is heading for the pan, what with this stuff in the news and the negative attitude of the UN. ZENDUST is gold but DARC is up shit creek without a paddle, or, if you like, without a company like SGB."

Kent knew he was right; DARC was finished, but ZENDUST was gold dust.

"We have plans for a ZENDUST Plus, but not with DARC's name anywhere near it. We are offering to acquire DARC Inc as a company, and you will be compensated. At the moment, looking at the New York Stock Exchange, we can buy DARC for peanuts. Your alternative is to liquidate the company, but you would lose Dr Douglas. You have no options, in reality."

Kent was a businessman, he knew DARC was finished, it was a do-or-die moment to make money from DARC.

"If you compensate me at yesterday's closing stock price, I will instruct our lawyers to contact you immediately."

Simons replied, "If we accept your offer, please understand that neither you nor anyone else from DARC, will have any position in the new ZENDUST Inc, company. We are already in direct contact with the Douglas family, and they want to work with SGB. Is that clear?"

Kent knew when to throw in his chips, "Yes, I understand, and accept the deal; I own the majority of DARC so there will be no problems from DARC personnel."

"OK, our lawyers will be in touch directly, Mr Kent," and the phone went dead.

Chapter 28
Cracking Up!

Fernando Gomez was usually a very calm and contented man. Over the long years of his life, he had endured so many close encounters with death and disaster that very little fazed him. *Until ZENDUST arrived and that jumped-up little shit Carlo Carioli hadot us involved with that company DARC. Everything had been fine before.* Gomez produced millions of dollars' worth of crack cocaine from his Colombian estates which he then managed to export by various means, mostly illegal, to feed the ever-increasing demands from the USA and Europe.

"Now, look what's happened," he said to his young grandson, Santiago, as they were sitting in the evening sunshine looking out over the terraces of orange trees and white scented roses. "I told the Carioli family to be careful and not to risk our lives and businesses, but they have taken no notice.

"I will tell you now, Santiago, something which I have kept hidden from you because I know you to be wild and hot-headed sometimes, which has caused us trouble. You are a young man, and I understand. I was hot-headed and wild when I was eighteen, just as you are now. You must now know that I believe the Carioli family to be responsible for the death of your father, Rico. I have kept this from you, because Rico was dead and there was nothing I could do about it. I have kept your father Rico in my mind though, every day. I knew the moment would come to settle this blood debt the Carioli family owe to our family Gomez. The moment is coming, and you will be the agent. But I don't want another death in our family so we must plan and be careful. Choosing the moment is what we must think about.

"I know you have been busy making sure our customers get the stuff they want, that the quality is good, and ensuring we are paid on time, but now is the time to make sure you understand everything that has gone on with that ZENDUST, Carioli and the American company DARC. You will see why I have kept things from you, and why we will settle the matter of your father and Carlo Carioli.

"ZENDUST looked like it was going to kill our business by stopping addiction so our customers would not want our cocaine. The DARC company needed money to put ZENDUST into production. That smartarse Carlo Carioli had the idea that the Carioli family would give DARC that money. They, like us, have a great deal of money that must be laundered and used, and I agreed that our family Gomez would join Carioli. ZENDUST has proved so popular that the daughter of the guy who developed it had the notion that it was OK to take the drug and then ZENDUST to cancel out any after-effects. We had that girl in our hands once but let her go at Carlo's request. Carlo had Rico killed to get his hands on the girl, whose name is Annie. Carioli's plan has failed; the company DARC is bankrupt and we have lost money. The girl is the cause of new ideas which must be eliminated, that is partly Carlo Carioli's fault because he fancies fucking her, and the inventor of ZENDUST has ruined our business so must be made to pay.

"Carlo Carioli has even been appearing at the United Nations with their boss Bom Patta saying that drugs should be legalised! Just think what would happen to us! The price would collapse and profit eliminated. He is no friend of ours.

"Santiago, do not be hasty, be careful, but take action, bring honour back to the Gomez family and save our business!"

"I will speak to Carioli and talk together, but he will get no hint of your plan, which you should not tell me."

"When you have executed your plan, I will know, and I will die in peace, for I am an old man and my life is nearly over."

"Yes, Grandfather. I understand everything. I know you have been honourable. I know what has been happening to us, driven by the Carioli family and the girl Annie Douglas and her father, who must be made to pay. I will leave you now and I will fulfil the

274

responsibilities of recovering the Gomez family honour and fortunes that you have placed upon me," and with that, he kissed his grandfather on both cheeks, held his hands, looked into his eyes, turned around and left the room.

Fernando Gomez watched Santiago leave the room, crossed himself, and prayed for the time he would see his grandson again.

After a few minutes, he picked up the phone and dialling Carlo Carioli, said, "This is Fernando Gomez. I see there is a big problem which we must discuss. Call me!" and put the phone down before Carioli could answer. He knew he would have to be very careful in talking to the Carioli family; he couldn't give any clue about what he had discussed with Santiago.

His phone lit up:

"Senor Gomez? This is Carlo Carioli; my father and I thank you for calling us. You will know that there is a problem with the American company DARC, but we want to tell you that your family will not lose any money because of your participation with us in the DARC project. Our family Carioli will make sure of that; we have millions of dollars available."

"Carlo, of course I am very shocked about what has happened as a result of your ideas for collaboration between our families on the DARC project and ZENDUST.

"I am very concerned that the possibility of our association with the Carioli family and DARC becoming public and featured in the news media. That is the most important thing. We have many customers for our cocaine who would not want the name of the Gomez family to be associated with your family and the DARC project in any way at all. Our customers are private and very nervous of media interference."

"Senor Gomez, I understand. The name of the Gomez family will never leave the lips of anyone in the Carioli family. If that happens, the person responsible will not live long."

"Carlo, we wish your family long life," and Fernando terminated the call.

As he cut the call, he knew that he wished Carlo a very short life, actually. The money was not important, the Gomez family was very wealthy, but those two, the Douglas man and his daughter Annie, must be made to pay for the trouble they had caused the Gomez business.

The most important thing was ensuring that the Carioli family paid the debt due to the Gomez family for the killing of Rico.

Fernando Gomez would now sit and wait for Santiago to fulfil this task.

Chapter 29
Fulfilment

Annie was thrilled with the way things were turning out. DARC had gone bankrupt but SGB and her friend Luke Simons had taken over the business and everything connected with ZENDUST. SGB had even been able to rescue her father from the laboratory where Solomons of DARC had banished him.

Annie was delighted to get rid of Solomons and DARC, especially after the drug connection had been revealed in the media and the treatment they had meted out to her father; after all, without him, DARC would never have made any money.

Annie had even been able to speak to her father and remembered that it had been a difficult conversation. *Dad had really blamed me for starting to use drugs after his ZENDUST had taken away the danger and then my going on TV telling all about my new campaign to legitimise all hard-core drugs, not to mention the 'Flowering of Freedom' campaign and the website* www.havefunwithZENDUST.com.

Thinking it all over again, she recalled that she had said, "You should know, Dad. That stuff in the news had been completely the opposite of my messages about the curse of drug addiction."

"Oh, Annie," John had replied, "ZENDUST has meant everything to me, probably much more that it should have done. I know now. It was me and my obsession that led Val, my darling wife, your lovely kind mum, to think I had forgotten her. You had vanished, but I didn't really know or care what had happened to you at that time. I was a star, everyone in the world wanted to hear from me. It was a merry-go-round that I didn't want to get off. Can you understand, if not forgive?"

Tears were forming in Annie's eyes as she thought back to that conversation. She had called her dad again, saying "Dad, I have also thought much more about what has happened. I realise now that I have wronged you and all your work on ZENDUST by giving it a life which you did not imagine but which will ultimately achieve what you wanted so much, the relief of the evils and exploitation of drug addiction. It just will not happen as you expected. I am so sorry for the hurt I have caused you. Mum has gone now, and thank God, she never had to know about my personal addiction and me going on the game… that would have killed her as effectively as you did by abandoning her for ZENDUST. I am so sorry, Dad, can you forgive me?"

John had been just as emotional, he loved his daughter. beyond measure, and simply said, "Of course Annie, all is forgiven, it's a new life ahead for both of us, I love you, Annie"

"I love you too, Dad."

Now, incredibly, John and Annie were about to take centre stage at a press conference organised not by DARC as before, but by SGB Pharmaceuticals to launch their new partnership. Bom Patta would be there, the General Secretary of the UN. Luke Simons knew this was news with a capital N. For John Douglas, this was déjà vu; this was the same hotel, and he was feeling the same nervousness and excitement that he experienced the first time around. The same vast audience from media throughout the world, the same good news to proclaim but this time, even better, he had Annie by his side.

After this press conference was over, John knew he would be ready to embark on a new life, a Zen-like life, without the obsessions of the past but with the peace and tranquillity of knowing that he had made a difference to the world. A new life he would now share with Annie. He had quit XTech as soon as he had put the phone down after talking to Annie

Luke called his room. "John, are you OK? In ten minutes? I will make the announcements on behalf of SGB and then introduce you and Annie, OK?"

"Yes, I'm fine, I will pick up Annie from her room next door," John said.

On stage, the media lights flickered for live transmission; the packed audience waited and governments worldwide tuned in. Luke Simons had ensured that there would be no taint of any association with the DARC or that investment outfit JC Investments who had, it turned out, got the money from shipping illegal cocaine in the first place. The audience had been carefully picked; Luke had made sure Carlo Carioli had been banned, but he was there backstage, having bribed the TV staff.

Jonah sat quietly at the back of the room, looking back on when he met Annie and everything that had happened since then. Life was very strange... Who would have thought it would be Annie up there...

Luke began. "Ladies and gentlemen, we are here today to launch the new partnership between SGB, Annie and John Douglas. This collaboration is targeted at turning ZENDUST into the solution for the illegal drug problems worldwide which have bedevilled and blighted countless lives. I know that you all heard a similar statement and hopes for the future at this podium when the DARC company launched ZENDUST last year. What nobody knew then, was that DARC used illegal funds from the illegal drugs industry. SGB has subsequently acquired the rights to ZENDUST and there is no taint to our money and our plans. We know John Douglas was innocent of any wrongdoing, and we know Anne Douglas is the inspiration for our new programme, which we will conduct with the aid and cooperation of the United Nations UNZAP project initiated by Annie Douglas.

"Unlike last time, this is a new dawn. ZENDUST will be sprinkled everywhere to the good of all mankind, and not for the profit of the few."

That soundbite went around the world in seconds, this was the real deal, ZENDUST would be the salvation, and everyone knew that SGB had the finance and capability to ensure success.

"Now, please let me introduce the stars of this project, father and daughter, John and Annie Douglas!"

Backstage, John took Annie's hand, they kissed briefly to recognise that they were together again, and walked forward into the bright lights...

As they walked forward, Santiago Gomez knew this was the moment he had been waiting for. He emerged from the shadows of backstage, pulled out his handgun, stepped up behind John and Annie, aimed at their heads and pulled the trigger, *POP* once, *POP* twice, the silenced gun spoke. John and Annie swayed forward in perfect unison and collapsed.

Carlo Carioli watched Santiago shoot John Douglas and Annie, thinking, *So that's it for them, they probably had it coming. It's a pity, I could have loved that Annie, but I know who Santiago's real target is.*

He stepped forward towards Santiago Gomez, who turned towards him and smiled, saying, "I knew you would be here Carlo; this is our gift to you." Aiming his gun directly at Carlo Cariolis heart he continued. "This is for Rico and our family honour," he pulled the trigger again, this time twice to be sure of Carlo's death, and stepped sideways into the gloom of backstage, sending a message on his phone to his grandfather, *"All is completed, in accordance with your wishes."* He disappeared down the back stairs into a waiting black limousine.

Out front, there was a horrified silence at what had been seen on TV across the world. The world was too shocked to move.

In Medellín, Fernando Gomez watched on TV, received the text message he had been waiting for and knew then that Santiago had made sure the Carioli family had paid their debt and that the Gomez family honour was satisfied. He relaxed on the sofa; this moment was his fulfilment. Then he went out to prune the roses.

John and Annie Douglas lay shot, holding hands, facing each other, the reconciliation of father and daughter in bloody togetherness, gazing at each other with love, and sorrow; after all the problems of their lives, apart; but now together, knowing that Val, as wife to John and mother to Annie, would be waiting to celebrate with them both a heavenly reconciliation, all else to be forgotten; the sound of sirens drew nearer, there seemed to be a bright light, it was so close...